The br(

Chapter 1 ·

The gates groaned open like old jaws. Steel scraped steel, slow and heavy. The air outside smelled like wet concrete and diesel. Adrian Marku stepped out alone, hands tucked into a bomber jacket issued by the prison, collar turned up against the rain. His boots were prison-polished, scuffed anyway. His eyes scanned the grey strip of road like he was searching for an ambush, not a ride.

Belmarsh didn't wave goodbye. It never did.

Behind him, a guard lit a cigarette under the awning and said, "Try not to come back, yeah?"

Ade didn't respond. He just walked. Four measured steps to the outer gate. Five to the sidewalk. Rain ticked on the shoulders of his coat. He breathed in shallow — like deeper air might choke him.

And then it came.

A scream of revving engine, sudden and out of place. The gates hadn't even finished clanking shut behind him when a white Lamborghini Urus slid up to the curb, almost fishtailing. The passenger window rolled down. Out popped a phone first — angled at him, recording — and then Kris Marku's voice:

"Ladies and gents! Guess who's back on the street? Big man's home!"

Ade squinted at the phone before he looked at his brother. Ten years gone, and the kid still grinned like he'd just pulled a prank.

Kris leaned across the passenger seat and pushed open the door. "Come on, bro. You don't wanna get caught on a bus looking like you just buried someone."

Ade didn't move.

"I said no cameras," he said, flat.

"No face, no case," Kris chirped. "It's not even live — yet."

He kept the phone trained as Ade stepped closer, slow and deliberate. Water dripped from his buzzcut. His eyes were unreadable — dark, calculating, not angry. Not yet.

Ade got in, slammed the door. The Lambo's interior glowed blue around them like a spaceship. Soft leather, fake luxury, reeked of new money and old mistakes.

Kris reversed with a grin.

"Belmarsh can suck it," he said. "We're back in business."

Ade stared ahead. "You smell like a nightclub toilet."

Kris laughed. "That's success, bruv."

Ade didn't smile. He just stared at the rain-glossed road as the prison shrank in the mirrors — then turned his face slightly, and muttered:

"You came late."

Kris blinked. "What?"

Ade finally looked at him. "You said noon. It's five."

Kris laughed nervously. "Traffic, man. Welcome to London."

Ade didn't reply. He looked out again. Rain smeared the windows. The city was waiting — and it looked nothing like he remembered.

"…You came late."

"You said noon. It's five."

Kris's nervous laugh still hung in the cabin like a bad cologne as they cut across a roundabout, tires screeching lightly on wet tarmac. Rain ran like tears down the windshield, caught in rhythmic wiper arcs.

Inside the Lamborghini, every surface glowed. Carbon fiber, LED trim, touchscreen maps. The soft bass of some trap remix throbbed under Kris's monologue. Ade sat low in the seat, body still, eyes scanning the road like a man waiting for the punchline of a joke no one told.

Kris kept talking.

"Bro. You gotta see the page. 18k followers since I teased the comeback last week. I said you were coming, not how or when, and boom — they're thirsty. They remember."

He flicked his phone on, not caring that he was driving. Flashing images. A logo: "BRUTALISTS / LONDON" overlaid on a grainy photo of Ade's 2009 mugshot.

"No face, no case, yeah, but this one's public record anyway," Kris said. "Made it look vintage. Like, retro. People eat that shit."

Ade didn't move. He didn't look at the phone. Outside, a kebab shop flickered by, its sign unreadable in the blur of rain. A boarded-up pub next. Then a freshly painted co-working space glowing like a medical ad.

"This isn't what I said," Ade said quietly.

Kris scoffed. "What, the logo? We can change it. But we gotta brand it now before someone else does. You were folklore for ten years. No TikTok, no videos. Just stories. You're like f—ing Bigfoot."

"You're talking to me like I'm a product."

Kris rolled his eyes. "Come on. No one remembers anyone who kept their head down. You want territory? Influence? You need narrative. You don't just take power now. You stream it."

Ade turned toward him, slowly.

"You're still a child," he said.

Kris's jaw twitched. "I'm the one who kept the name alive while you were rotting in Belmarsh."

They drove in silence for a few moments.

The Lambo rolled past a line of hoardings painted with bright colors and developers' promises: URBAN REVIVAL – LUXURY LIVING COMING SOON. Behind them: skeletons of half-finished flats, cranes like broken limbs against the sky.

A sharp turn. Then — the old neighborhood.

Concrete towers, faded grime-smeared paint, small gangs of kids in puffers hunched around vape smoke. The rain hadn't touched them. The place felt preserved in damp rage.

Kris slowed.

"To the left," he said, pointing. "Look."

A wall mural — five meters high, cleanly painted, stylized. Reggie and Ronnie Kray in black and white suits, flanked by bulldogs and roses. Gold crowns airbrushed above their heads.

Kris beamed. "Iconic, right?"

Ade stared at it.

Nothing.

Kris waited for a reaction. Got none. Just the sound of rain. Just the rumble of the engine and the steady click of the blinker.

Ade leaned forward slightly.

"They died in cages," he said flatly. "You want that? Go paint your own face on a wall."

Kris didn't answer.

The Lambo pulled away in silence, slick and slow, past tower blocks, shuttered bookies, and chicken shops glowing under CCTV glare.

Behind them, the mural faded into the mist — a myth made sterile by paint.

The Lambo slowed outside a narrow storefront tucked between a betting shop and a vape lounge. A flickering sign above the awning read KAFENË E SHQIPONJËS — the eagle café. The windows were fogged with condensation and grease. A man in a flat cap was passed out at one of the outside tables, untouched espresso in front of him, a cigarette burning to the filter.

Kris parked half on the curb, killed the engine. The silence was louder than the motor.

"Don't say anything about the smell," Kris muttered as they climbed the stairwell.

"Wasn't planning to," Ade said.

The stairwell was concrete, painted a nicotine-stained cream. Old flyers curled on the walls. The smell hit halfway up — not rot exactly, but feathers, shit, and bleach. At the top floor, a door hung open slightly. Pigeons cooed beyond it.

Ade stepped through.

The flat was small, dim, and full of ghosts.

Wire cages lined one wall, each holding two or three pigeons. A low table was stacked with empty whiskey bottles, yellowed newspapers, and a cracked radio muttering in Albanian. On the wall: black-and-white photos of young men with rifles in the mountains. Beside them, a faded portrait of the Marku brothers' father — jaw like a cliff face, arms folded, eyes angry even in stillness.

Uncle Ermal Marku — Ermi — sat in an old recliner with one foot wrapped in a bandage and an unlit cigar wedged in the side of his mouth. He didn't move when they entered.

"You're late," he said, eyes still on the birds.

"Traffic," Kris muttered. "And Belmarsh took their time."

Ade stood still by the doorway. Ermi looked up, squinted, and grunted.

"You look the same. Bit more skull showing, maybe."

Ade didn't smile.

"Your door was open."

"I don't lock it. Anyone wants me dead that bad, they'll kick it in anyway."

He finally stood — slowly — and limped across the room, hand out. Ade took it. The grip was strong for a man who looked like a pensioner who'd been fighting gravity for a decade.

"You hungry?" Ermi asked. "I got bread, fish, some piss-poor whiskey."

"No."

"You will be."

Kris dropped onto the couch like it owed him rent. "I told you he'd come out lean. Guy was doing pushups on concrete floors, eating oatmeal, reading Machiavelli or some shit."

"I read nothing," Ade said.

Ermi chuckled and sat again. A pigeon fluttered in a cage behind him. "You read the wall," he said. "That's what prison teaches you. How to watch the wall."

Ade stepped to the window. From here, you could see across rooftops — to cranes, towers, half-demolished estates. The city looked like it was eating itself alive.

He said, "What happened to Milo?"

Ermi's eyes darkened. "Dead."

"Who?"

Kris answered. "Guy who used to run the fight nights under the tunnels. Got stabbed last year. Someone said it was for unpaid coke but—"

"Shut up," Ermi snapped. "It wasn't coke. It was because he didn't know when to shut his mouth."

Ade nodded. "And Dezi?"

"Gone straight. Owns a mechanic shop in Barking. Wears golf shirts now. Doesn't return calls."

"And Dritan?"

Ermi looked at the pigeons. "You don't want to know."

Ade turned back to him. "I need a crew."

"You had one."

"I need a new one."

Ermi leaned forward, poured a finger of brown from a chipped bottle into a shot glass, but didn't drink. "Most of the old boys are either ghosts or cowards. You want to build again, you build with kids. But kids don't build. They burn."

He tilted the shot back. Winced.

"You see that estate across the road?" Ermi nodded out the window. "Used to be ours. You could walk from the top floor to the pavement and shake twenty loyal hands. Now? One call from a middle manager at some security firm and you're out on your arse."

Kris lit a cigarette.

"We're gonna take that back," he said, blowing smoke toward the ceiling. "One block at a time."

Ermi said nothing.

Ade looked down at the table. A photo, tucked between two coasters — the three of them, a decade ago. Before the blood. Before the gates.

His voice was quiet.

"We don't take it back. We bury what's there. Then we build something worse."

Ermi nodded, tired eyes sharp.

"Then start digging."

"Then start digging," Ermi had said.

So they did — not with shovels, but with silence. The room hung heavy with old names and older absences. Kris broke the moment first.

"I've got something I want to show you," he said, flicking the cigarette into an empty coffee cup. "Been working on it while you were still inside."

Ade followed him out. Back through the rank stairwell, back into the damp slap of East London air. The Lambo was still there, fogged windows, one headlight blinking — like it knew it didn't belong.

They didn't speak much on the drive. Kris tuned the radio to something bass-heavy, then muted it halfway through the track. The streets thickened with traffic as they cut deeper into the borough. Tower blocks rose like tired giants, graffiti scarring their ankles. The estate they arrived at had no name anymore — just a postcode that scared off delivery drivers.

The tower was thirteen floors high, half its windows blown out or boarded up. Rats would've thought twice about moving in.

Kris parked and killed the engine.

"Recognise it?" he said.

Ade studied the building. The balconies sagged. A sheet of corrugated metal had been nailed across the main door. In the side alley, kids were sharing balloons and energy drinks, barely glancing at the car. The building looked abandoned. It wasn't.

"No cameras," Kris said. "No law. Just watchers. Lenny's boys, mostly. Albanian-lite. They use the flats to cut pills and do drop-offs. Stash points in the lift shafts. Nothing heavy. Just enough to keep them visible."

Ade's eyes narrowed.

"And?"

"I want it. First move. Symbolic."

Ade said nothing.

Kris continued, "You take one tower, you send a message. You don't have to fight ten wars when the first shot's clean. These lot think they're untouchable. Everyone's scared to make noise. But they're lazy. Flashy. No roots."

Ade finally stepped out of the car. His boots hit the wet concrete like punctuation.

He stood still for a moment, staring up at the building like it had just insulted him. Then he walked toward it. Not fast. Not slow. Deliberate. Kris scrambled to follow.

They moved past a half-lit stairwell where someone had dumped a broken scooter. Up the fire escape — rusted steps groaning under their weight. Third floor. The air stank of piss, fried oil, and burnt plastic.

Kris nudged a door open with his foot. Inside, the flat was stripped bare — just a mattress, cracked tiles, tagging on the walls. One word stood out, sprayed large over the far window: "FAME."

Kris chuckled. "Poetic, innit?"

Ade didn't answer. He walked to the balcony.

The city stretched out before them, cracked and glowing — glass towers rising like blades above crooked estates. The skyline looked like it was arguing with itself.

Ade leaned on the rusted railing. Rain beaded on his shaved scalp.

Kris joined him, arms folded. "Imagine it. Cleaned up. Tinted windows. Whole floor turned into a cash safe, ops running out the basement. We stream the takeover, anonymised masks, blackout camera — like a f—ing action short film. Whole of TikTok watching live while we take back London."

Ade still didn't speak.

Kris looked sideways. "You seeing it?"

"No," Ade said.

Kris blinked. "What?"

"I'm seeing a graveyard. Just don't know whose yet."

The wind picked up. Somewhere below, a dog barked.

Ade's voice was lower now, the kind that didn't need volume to hit like a hammer.

"This city don't need gangsters. It needs ghosts. Quiet ones. The kind that slip between cracks and don't leave evidence."

Kris laughed nervously. "You sound like Ermi."

Ade didn't laugh. He kept watching the lights.

"I sound like someone who's been inside a decade. Watching men pretend they're gods, then cry when the doors close."

He turned to face his brother.

"You wanna build something real? Then bury the show. Or you're dead before we start."

For once, Kris had no clever comeback.

He just nodded, slow. But his eyes didn't agree.

The rain followed them back to the café flat like a loyal curse.

Inside, the lights hummed dim and yellow. The pigeons rustled in their cages. Uncle Ermi snored on the recliner with a blanket over his lap and an empty shot glass balanced on his chest. One of the birds cooed rhythmically, like a bored metronome.

Kris was on the sofa, phone in hand, scrolling furiously. His face lit up with dopamine-glazed approval.

"Four thousand views in under an hour. Comments are fire. 'Real ones are back', 'London ain't been the same since Ade left', 'Someone tag Netflix'. Even got a DM from a grime artist. Wants to use the footage for a track intro."

He flipped the screen toward Ade, who stood by the kitchen counter, arms crossed. On the screen: a shaky vertical video of Belmarsh's gates swinging open. Ade stepping out. Kris's excited voice narrating: "Ladies and gents, he's out. He's back. Ade Marku returns."

The caption was big, bold, and stupid:

#THEBRUTALISTS

Ade didn't move.

"You filmed me walking," he said flatly.

"Yeah," Kris said, like it was obvious. "It's the moment, bro. We needed a moment. It's not like I showed your face properly. It's all shadows and posture. It's art."

"I told you not to film me."

"You said no livestream. This wasn't live."

Ade took a slow step forward.

Kris raised his hands, chuckling. "Bro. It's out there now. Deleting it makes us look scared. You've got people talking. They're remembering."

Ade's jaw clenched.

"I don't want to be remembered," he said. "I want to be feared."

Kris paused. "Fear don't trend."

Ermi stirred in the recliner.

"You two arguing again?" he muttered without opening his eyes.

Kris rolled his eyes. "Just creative differences."

Ermi opened one eye and squinted at the phone still glowing in Kris's hand.

"You filming your brother like he's a monkey in a suit?"

"It's marketing."

Ermi sat up slowly, bones cracking. He reached for his bottle, changed his mind, and pointed instead.

"You know who else loved cameras? The Krays. Took pictures with celebrities, politicians, even f—ing boxers. Smiled big. Thought they were untouchable."

Ade watched him closely.

Ermi continued, "You know what I remember about them most? That photo they took outside the club. Ronnie in the coat, Reggie with the ring. Real sharp. Looked like kings. That photo hung in every paper after the trial."

He leaned forward.

"Now you tell me — was that their legacy? Or was that their f—ing eulogy?"

The room fell still.

Kris's face tightened, but he didn't answer. He just looked back at the screen, then tucked the phone away — like maybe that put the video back in its box.

Ade turned to Ermi. Voice low, steady.

"You think we can't do it different?"

Ermi snorted. "I think if you try to dance in two worlds — fame and fear — you fall between. One gets you money. The other gets you respect. Neither keeps you alive."

Kris muttered something under his breath.

"What?" Ade asked.

Kris looked up. "I said maybe we don't need to live forever. Maybe it's enough to matter while we're here."

Ade stared at him.

Ermi reached for the birds, opened a cage, and let one out. It fluttered awkwardly onto his wrist.

"Either you kill this early," he said, staring at the pigeon, "or it kills both of you."

The bird cocked its head. The silence stretched.

Outside, the rain thickened — but London didn't care. It pulsed and burned and watched, like it always had.

Chapter 2 - Bricks and teeth

"You want it clean," Ade said. "Then listen."

The table in the café's back room was covered with a rough sketch of the tower block: stairwells, floor numbers, door markings. Coffee rings stained the edges, and a half-burnt cigarette balanced on a saucer sent up a lazy trail of smoke.

"Two stairwells," he continued, pointing with a pen that had been chewed down to its plastic nerves. "One working lift, always stuck on five. Entry through the back corridor — avoid the courtyard, it's got eyes."

Kris nodded, but his leg bounced. He was scrolling through his second phone, the one with no contact name, just icons and encrypted threads.

"We do floor-by-floor, yeah?" Kris said. "Film it masked, edit later, add distortion — like one of those urban legend videos. Cuts between doors going down, silent shots, black hoodies. You seen the 'Ghost Blocks' series on YouTube?"

Ade didn't look up.

"I said listen."

Kris froze.

Ade's voice stayed calm. Controlled.

"You want spectacle. Fine. You get one camera. One shooter. Someone you trust. No ego shots. No names. No laughing. No f—ing slow-motion edits."

He tapped the stairwell again.

"This isn't a video. It's a message."

Kris nodded slowly. "Got it."

Ermi watched from the doorway, lighting another cigarette. The light caught his tired eyes, flickering like a dying TV screen.

"Messages go both ways," he said. "You hit a place like that, someone answers. Maybe not today. Maybe not tomorrow. But someone always answers."

Kris glanced up. "Let 'em. That's the point."

Ermi blew smoke toward the pigeons in the corner, locked away for the night.

"Boys used to think like that before they stopped coming home."

Ade looked at him. "You still have the bolt cutters?"

"In the cupboard. Next to the plum brandy you're not allowed to drink yet."

Ade folded the paper map, tucked it into his coat pocket. Then he grabbed the burner phone Kris had handed him earlier — no contacts, just camera and notes — and dropped it into the inside lining.

"You'll take the left stairwell with two," Ade said to Kris. "I'll take the right with the others. We move at the same pace. No blood, no shouting, no damage except doors and burners."

"No blood," Kris repeated.

"Say it like you believe it."

Kris met his eyes. "No blood."

Ade nodded once.

Ermi didn't move from the doorway. "If I hear sirens," he said, "I'm locking the door. You're both just two lads from the estate who got into a fight with shadows. And I don't know either of you."

Kris grinned. "Don't worry, Unc. By morning, we'll be trending."

Ade adjusted his coat, stepped past Ermi, and opened the door to the alley.

Rain was still falling.

"You're already trending," Ermi muttered.

"No," Ade said, stepping into the dark. "We're just starting.

"We're just starting."

The alley swallowed Ade's words as he stepped into the night, the hood of his coat already beading with rain. Kris followed close behind, his breath sharp in the cold. Three others trailed them — all younger, dressed in black, faces wrapped in cheap cotton balaclavas. One held a bolt cutter. Another gripped a crowbar with his name scratched into the handle. The third carried nothing but a burner phone duct-taped to a chest mount. Silent. Ready.

The estate loomed ahead — thirty years of piss-stained concrete and broken windows. Its stairwells lit by a sick yellow glow. The ground floor smelled of wet chip paper, stale weed, and ammonia. Bin fires burned in oil drums around the back corner, giving everything a carnival-horror flicker.

Ade raised a hand. They stopped just outside the rear service entrance.

"Last check," he said.

No one spoke. Only nods.

Kris adjusted the mask covering his lower face and pulled his hood up tight. He vibrated with energy, like he was about to go on stage.

Ade turned the knob on the torch duct-taped to his own chest. It blinked once. No beam — just infrared. Night vision was for amateurs. This was about movement, not visibility.

He handed Kris a battered radio. "You go left. I go right. Sweep up to seven. Hit top floor together."

"Ten-minute sweep?"

"Fifteen. Don't run. If anyone fights, leave them breathing. That was the rule."

Kris smirked under the mask. "No blood. I know."

Ade stared a moment longer, then kicked the bottom corner of the door.

The latch cracked. The door groaned open.

They moved inside.

The hallway was narrow, tiled in grime. Graffiti crawled across the ceiling like mold. Doorbells buzzed faintly, as if warning each other. From above, faint music pulsed — distorted grime leaking through thin floors.

They split.

Ade and the two kids took the right stairwell. Boots on concrete. No words. No eye contact. Just the rhythmic echo of footfalls and the hiss of quiet breath under fabric.

First floor: empty. Smelled of burnt rubber. A broken scooter lay in the corridor like a carcass.

Second floor: movement. A kid in a red puffa jacket saw them, froze, and bolted down the hall. Didn't even scream. Just vanished.

Ade paused by a door, pressed his gloved hand against the paint. Warm. Someone inside, maybe cooking, maybe sleeping. He moved on.

Third floor.

A tripwire across the stairwell.

He saw it too late.

One of the kids clipped it — a can dropped from the ceiling, clanging down the stairs. Loud. Metal on concrete. Then — silence.

Ade didn't flinch. He crouched, held a finger to his lips. Listened.

Breath.

Not theirs.

Faint, sharp. Behind the door to his right. A wheeze, a step.

Then the door burst open — and the man came out swinging.

Small. Fast. Blade in hand.

The kid with the crowbar jumped back. The cameraman nearly dropped the phone.

Ade didn't.

He moved in — not fast, but heavy, precise.

One hand grabbed the man's wrist. The other drove forward like a piston — into the man's throat.

Not a punch. A shove. Knuckles to trachea.

The blade clattered.

The man dropped to the floor, gagging, kicking weakly.

Ade stood over him, silent.

The kids stared.

"You okay?" the crowbar kid finally asked.

Ade didn't answer. He bent down, picked up the knife, snapped the blade from the handle, and tossed both pieces in opposite directions.

The man wheezed. Tried to rise.

Ade put a boot on his chest. Pressed, not too hard. Just enough to remind him.

"Don't follow," he said.

Then he moved on.

No blood.

Just a broken sound left behind.

The body wheezed behind them as Ade's crew stepped over him, silent again.

On the sixth floor, the stairwell smelled like sweat and cheap aftershave — someone had been through here recently, fast. The silence above wasn't calm; it was waiting.

Kris's voice crackled in Ade's earpiece.

"Seventh. Right corridor. Light's on. Feels hot."

Ade raised a hand. His two runners paused behind him. He reached into his coat and pulled a tiny EMP puck — black, scratched, about the size of a coaster. He pressed it flat to the junction box beside the lift. It clicked once.

The lights above snapped out.

Darkness.

Then: pounding footsteps across the floor above them. Shouts. Slams.

Ade and the crew took the last flight in a rush.

At the landing, one door stood slightly ajar. A dull blue glow inside. Cigarette smoke leaking through the crack.

Ade nodded once.

The crowbar kid stepped forward and kicked.

The door cracked open — just enough.

Ade followed through, hard.

The flat was lit only by a TV playing static and a strip of LEDs behind the sofa. Four men jumped up — one with a burner, one with a half-smoked blunt, the others scrambling for something under the coffee table.

They didn't make it.

Ade moved first.

He took the one with the burner — snapped the gun from his hand and cracked it across his jaw. The man dropped.

The second guy bolted toward the kitchen. The crowbar caught his knee mid-run.

Screams. Chaos. Fast.

Kris's crew burst in seconds later — phones mounted to chests, faces hidden. One camera caught the wide shot: masked figures flooding the flat, shadows darting in LED glow. A hooded kid smashed the burner phones on the table with the back of a hammer. Another tipped a cheap desktop tower out the window.

Ade grabbed the one in charge — shirtless, gold chain, shaven head, eyes wide.

He slammed him against the kitchen counter. Open palm, not fist. Didn't want blood — but he wanted a bruise.

"You know who we are?" Ade said, calm.

The man nodded.

"You know what this is?"

Another nod. Quieter.

"You say our names, it's your last word. You breathe our names, you never breathe again."

The man coughed, nodded again.

Kris stepped into the shot. Just for a second. Hands behind his back, stance wide. Then he disappeared back into the hallway.

Ade let the man slide to the floor.

"Leave."

The guy didn't hesitate. Crawled toward the door, one hand to his cheek.

"Anything worth keeping?" Ade called.

Kris answered from the bedroom. "Stash is low. Probably already moved it. But I left a gift."

Ade raised an eyebrow.

The bedroom door swung open. On the bed, Kris had left a single red hoodie — folded perfectly, center pillow. On top: a burner phone, camera still running.

"What's on it?"

Kris smiled behind his mask. "Us."

Ade stared a second longer — then walked out.

By the time they reached the car, Kris had already cut a teaser from the raw footage. Just fifteen seconds.

Black screen. Then: a door kicked in. A face blurred. A phone smashed.

Overlay:

THE BRUTALISTS. FLOOR BY FLOOR.

Uploaded to three burner accounts. Timed to drop on rotation, ten minutes apart.

By the time they pulled away, the first post already had two hundred comments.

The kettle screamed.

Ermi shut it off before it boiled over. Steam hissed out of the spout as he poured water into two chipped mugs, both stained from years of heavy use. One read "WORLD'S OKAYEST UNCLE." The other was plain white, cracked around the handle.

On the TV, muted, a football match played to no one. Above it, pinned to the wall with a bit of old chewing gum, was a yellowed photo of Ermi and the Marku brothers' father — both younger, both mean-looking, both holding cans of beer like they were medals.

The phone buzzed.

It was Kris's.

Ermi glanced at the screen. Burner account notification. Over a thousand likes. Comments piling in.

"Where is this?"

"REAL SHIT."

"Bruv that's the flats near Stepney, no?"

"Old school's BACK."

"Brutalists run East again"

Ermi shook his head and took a sip of tea.

The door creaked.

Ade walked in, slow, silent. His right hand was red — not bleeding, but raw. Knuckles scuffed and purpling. He walked past the couch without a word, past the table, and into the little kitchenette. He turned on the tap. Cold. Let the water run.

Ermi didn't say anything for a moment. Then:

"You hit a man?"

Ade didn't look back. "He pulled a blade."

"You could've talked."

"No time."

"You could've left it."

Ade scrubbed the blood from his hand with dish soap and a cloth that should've been thrown out last year. He didn't scrub fast. He wasn't trying to be clean. Just trying to be done.

Ermi muttered, "You always choose pain."

Ade dried his hand, slowly.

"Only when it speaks louder than words."

From the hallway, Kris's voice called out:

"Oi, Ermi — you seen the Twitter reaction yet?"

Ermi called back without turning. "Just saw it. You'll get your movie deal in no time."

Kris appeared, hoodie off, smiling wide. "It's better than I thought. Three reposts, and the YouTube cut's already hit a thousand. They're calling us the new wave."

Ade looked at him — but didn't say a word.

Kris tossed him a can from the fridge. "You earned that. You did good."

Ade caught it, didn't open it.

"You post the footage from the flat?" he asked.

"Only a teaser," Kris said. "Blurred faces, chopped audio. Don't worry. We're ghosts."

Ade raised an eyebrow. "Ghosts don't upload."

Kris grinned, shrugged. "Ghosts evolve."

On the other side of London, Maya Khan lay on her bed with her laptop open and a cheap glass of red wine balanced on her stomach. She paused a podcast episode mid-edit to scroll Twitter. A retweet from an anonymous urban media account caught her eye: THE BRUTALISTS. FLOOR BY FLOOR.

She clicked.

Watched.

Leaned forward slowly, sipping her wine.

Then clicked again.

Then saved it.

Meanwhile, in a windowless office tucked behind a kebab shop police front, Detective Cal Lowry lit a cigarette with hands that trembled slightly from too much coffee and not enough sleep. His phone pinged. Private contact. A still frame of the teaser. Time-stamped, blurred.

He muttered under his breath, dragged deep on the cigarette, and picked up the phone.

"Yeah," he said. "I saw it. Send me the original file. And get someone to scrape metadata."

Pause.

"No. Not again. Not these f—ing clowns. We buried this once already."

He hung up.

At the café, Ade sat at the table with the can still unopened in front of him. Kris paced, giddy. Planning the next one already — a second estate, tighter edit, live feed with a coded map drop. Audience interaction.

Ade didn't interrupt.

Didn't say a word.

But his knuckles were still purple.

And his silence was getting louder.

Dawn slid in under the smog like a thief — dim and indifferent, washing the streets in cold ash-light. The rain had stopped hours ago, but the pavement still sweated moisture. Somewhere, the muffled wail of an ambulance gave up chasing anything and faded into silence.

Ermi stepped out the café's back door in his slippers, expecting only a piss and the first cigarette of the day. He lit the smoke before he noticed it.

Nailed to the middle of the doorframe — not tacked, not hung, nailed — was a dead pigeon.

Its wings were spread wide, twisted like they'd been pulled into that position. Its belly had been sliced open. The guts were mostly gone, but a half-smoked cigarette had been tucked inside its beak like a joke. The nail went straight through its chest.

Ermi didn't move for a moment.

Then he exhaled smoke through his nose and muttered:

"Shqyer n'dysh."

He left the door ajar and went back inside.

Ade was already up. He sat at the kitchen table, not moving, same spot he'd ended the night. A cigarette smoldered in the ashtray. The unopened beer still beside it.

"You up?" Ermi asked.

Ade didn't answer.

"I've got something."

Ade looked at him. Not fast. Just lifted his gaze.

Ermi tilted his head toward the alley.

Ade stood. No words.

They walked to the back.

Ade looked once. That was enough.

He studied the way the wings had been spread. The angle of the nail. The cigarette in the beak.

Ermi watched him. "Lenny?"

Ade nodded.

"Could be the kids from the estate trying to—"

"No," Ade said. "Too clean."

He crouched beside it, staring at the thing like it was a map. The wings were twisted, not broken. The placement was surgical.

"This is someone showing they know us," he said.

"Or that they want us to think they do."

"Same thing."

Behind them, Kris's voice yawned into the hallway.

"What's going on?"

He stepped out, rubbing his eyes, barefoot, hoodie hanging off one shoulder.

Then he saw it.

He recoiled half a step, blinked.

"Jesus."

"No," Ermi said. "Just Lenny."

Kris looked between them. "You sure?"

Ade didn't look at him. "Yeah."

Kris squinted at the bird, then smirked faintly. "What, we getting into pagan shamanic warfare now?"

Ermi muttered, "You joke when you don't understand."

Kris shrugged. "You've got pigeons upstairs. Should I worry they're working both sides?"

Ade stood. He was quiet. His hands slid into his coat pockets.

"This isn't a threat," he said. "It's a courtesy."

Kris frowned. "How's that better?"

"It means we're on the board. They're not ignoring us."

Kris leaned against the wall. "So what, we film a reply? Get a rooster and shove a cigar up its arse?"

Ermi turned to him. "You want to die funny or live quiet?"

Kris didn't answer. He just scratched his chin and turned back inside.

But once he was in the hallway, out of their view, he pulled out his phone and opened a contact he hadn't messaged in weeks.

Maya Khan.

He typed:

Got something for you. Private. No cameras. Just talk.

You want to hear it first?

He hovered.

Then sent it.

Back outside, Ade watched the pigeon for a second longer, then reached up and gripped the nail.

Ermi winced. "What are you—?"

Ade ripped it free in one clean jerk. The pigeon dropped into a black bin bag.

"Don't leave gifts at the door," he said. "People start thinking it's welcome."

Chapter 3 - Modern Myth

RECORDING LIGHT ON.

Room tone. Buzzing fridge in the background. London traffic in the distance, faint and constant.

Maya's voice, low and deliberate, cuts in:

"This story doesn't start with a gunshot.

It starts with silence.

A door opening on a block in East London.

A man stepping out after ten years.

No entourage. No banner. Just one phone camera, already rolling.

And a name whispered under breath: Marku."

She hit pause.

Rewound the clip.

Played it again — the moment Ade stepped through Belmarsh's gates, the frame slightly shaky, the audio blown out by Kris's voice shouting "He's back!"

She didn't include Kris's voice in the podcast. Not yet.

Instead, she faded in ambient sounds: rain on concrete, echoing stairwell samples she'd recorded herself last week in Tower Hamlets. She layered it with a lo-fi bass line, gave the words space to breathe.

Maya sat back in her creaking chair, rubbing the scar at the corner of her jaw. Her flat was a nest of wires and notes — red string, sticky tabs, USB drives jammed in every outlet. Sound foam dulled the windows. A single microphone dangled over her workspace like a surgical light.

She clicked a different track: an interview she'd recorded with a sociology professor. Something about urban decay and the mythologizing of gangsters. She cut that, too. Saved it for later.

The real draw wasn't theory. It was blood. And brothers.

She picked up her mug. Cold coffee. She didn't care.

"Kris Marku," she said into the mic. "Younger. Flashier. The one smiling in every photo. The kind of man who knows exactly how to hold your gaze long enough to make you forget why you were looking in the first place.

He contacted me last week."

Click. Insert audio:

KRIS (RECORDED): "You want the truth, yeah? I'll give it to you raw. But only if you get it right. This ain't about crime. It's about legacy."

Back to Maya:

"He offered me something no one else had. Access. The inside track.

I said yes.

I met him at a basement bar in Shoreditch two days ago. Masked door. Private room. Two bouncers playing chess. The room smelled like citrus and cocaine."

She hit stop.

Reached into her pocket. Pulled out her notebook — dense with scribbles. She flipped to the page marked Kris – Bar Meeting.

— constantly checking his phone

— leather jacket (fake?)

— watched the bouncers watching me

— talked like he was narrating his own biopic

— said "legacy" six times

— asked if I "vibed" with violence

She pulled her laptop closer and opened the interview file. Kris's voice filled the room again, bouncing off the foam.

"See, people think gangsters are dumb. But we're storytellers. That's what fear is. A story you tell someone so they never test you. My brother? He doesn't get that. He is fear. I'm the f—ing narrator."

Maya smiled faintly. It wasn't a real smile. Just an instinct.

She clicked open her project timeline. Moved the voiceover file up, laid it over the stairwell ambiance. Then the track of the door getting kicked in. The teaser video's sound, filtered and distorted.

Ade's heavy boots. The low, muttered voice: "You breathe our names, you never breathe again."

She froze.

Listened again.

Rewound.

Let it sit.

Then hit record.

"Ade Marku. The older one. A shadow in a coat. A man who never blinks and never rushes. Some say he did ten years for a murder no one proved. Others say he kept quiet for someone else's crime. What I know is this — when he speaks, you listen.

And when he doesn't, you listen harder."

She stopped.

Sat back.

Saved the file as:

Episode One – The Brutalists

Draft A: Fear vs Fame

She reached for her phone.

A message from Kris was already there:

U good for tomorrow? Got something I want you to hear. Just us. No mics unless I say.

She stared at the message.

Then typed:

Sure. Time?

Kris replied instantly:

Midnight. Top floor. Bring ears. Not opinions.

Maya didn't smile. She just closed her laptop, flicked the light off, and sat in the dark.

Listening to Ade's voice echo again in her headphones.

You breathe our names, you never breathe again.

The elevator wheezed up six floors before groaning to a stop that felt like it might be permanent. Maya stepped out into a corridor that smelled like burnt foil and damp carpet. The top floor of the estate had been repurposed — not renovated, not cleaned, but claimed. The hallway buzzed faintly from an exposed light cable snaking along the ceiling. Someone had painted a crude logo on the wall outside the last door: BRUTALIST HQ in red spray paint, dripping like sarcasm.

She knocked.

The door opened halfway — then all the way, fast.

Kris stood there, wearing a crisp white tee, chain tucked just enough to be visible, and the kind of grin that was less about greeting and more about setting the tone.

"Maya Khan," he said. "Welcome to the kingdom."

She stepped inside.

The flat was… curated. Not cleaned. Not improved. Just arranged. One wall was plastered with screenshots of social media posts, a digital map with red pins across boroughs. A table covered in burner phones, empty cans of energy drink, and half-sketched logo ideas. A whiteboard read:

BRUTALIST = IMAGE + FEAR + STORY

✚ "Fear that films well"

✚ Control the aesthetic

✚ No old man energy

Maya arched an eyebrow. "No old man energy?"

Kris grinned, flicked a lighter open and shut. "Means we don't do what they did. No dusty suits, no pub backrooms. We brand the myth before someone else does. That's power now — narrative management."

"Sounds like PR."

"Exactly. But with machetes."

She walked slowly across the room, recording ambient sound on her phone — Kris's steps, the hum of a portable speaker, the flutter of a pigeon outside the cracked window. Everything was intentional, which meant everything was worth studying.

He gestured at a rack of hoodies with the Brutalist logo screen-printed in cheap ink.

"Limited run," he said. "Only fifty made. They sell out, we triple price next drop. Scarcity is credibility."

Maya tilted her head. "You're running a gang like a streetwear label."

Kris's grin sharpened. "You say that like it's a bad thing."

"I say that like I've seen four dozen boys sell branded balaclavas and end up stabbed in a stairwell."

Kris leaned against the wall, hands in pockets.

"We're not four dozen boys. We're Markus."

His voice dropped an octave — performing. He liked this part. The bit where he said something heavy, paused, let it hang like prophecy.

Maya didn't bite.

"You sound rehearsed," she said.

He blinked.

"I sound ready."

"No," she said. "You sound like you're waiting for a camera that isn't there."

He laughed — but it came out too fast, too defensive.

"I thought you wanted a story."

"I want the story."

He stepped closer. Not threatening. Just close.

"Then keep your mic off for a minute."

Maya didn't flinch. She turned off her recorder.

Kris dropped his voice. "You ever get that feeling you're in your own trailer? Like everything's cut for drama, every shot a setup?"

Maya narrowed her eyes. "You mean paranoia?"

"I mean prologue."

She didn't respond. Just looked at him — and behind him.

The bedroom door was ajar.

Inside, dark. Quiet.

A shape sitting in the corner. Still. Watching.

Ade.

Maya didn't move. Neither did he.

"You let her in?" Ade's voice, quiet, from the shadows.

Kris turned halfway, surprised. "Yeah. We said midnight."

"She recording?"

"No."

A pause. Ade's silhouette stayed still.

"Good."

Maya looked at Kris. "You didn't tell me he'd be here."

"I didn't tell him you would."

From the corner, a flick of a lighter. Brief light on Ade's face — gaunt, unreadable.

Then dark again.

Kris turned back to Maya with that smile again, soft this time.

"Like I said," he murmured. "Kingdom."

The smell hit first — sharp, warm, and unmistakably bird. Maya stepped into Uncle Ermi's flat with her scarf pulled slightly over her nose. Pigeons rustled in their cages, blinking at her like silent judges. The windows were fogged, and the room was orange with the kind of light that came from bulbs bought cheap and left on too long.

Ermi didn't rise. He was already seated at his usual throne: a battered recliner patched with duct tape and betrayal. His feet rested on an upside-down crate of imported soda. Cigarette burning down in one hand. Remote in the other.

"You're early," he said without looking at her.

"You said two," Maya replied.

"I say a lot of things."

He waved vaguely at the only other chair in the flat that wasn't hosting a birdcage or a growing pile of receipts.

She sat.

She pulled her mic out, clipped it to her coat, and said clearly:

"This is Maya Khan. I'm here with Ermal Marku, uncle to Ade and Kris Marku—"

He snorted. "Don't call me uncle on tape. Makes me sound cuddly."

She ignored him.

"…to talk about family, history, and the origin of the men now making headlines — or hashtags."

Ermi took a drag. Exhaled through his nose.

"You want stories, you gotta understand this city don't keep stories. It eats them. Swallows them down and spits up slogans."

"Then let's start before the slogans," Maya said.

Ermi smiled faintly. "You think you're clever."

"I think you're interesting."

"That's worse."

She waited. He didn't speak. Just stared at her, smoke curling around his face.

Then finally:

"Their dad — Valon — he was smart. Smarter than both of 'em, and that's saying something. Used to run with Serbs, Turks, even an Irish lot back in the late 80s. Knew when to smile, when to slit. Ran bookmaking out of butcher shops. Good cover — meat and money look the same in the wrong light."

Maya leaned forward. "And?"

"And he got greedy. Started talking legacy. Wanted to own things. Not just run 'em. Wanted buildings. Land. Respect with titles. But the East End don't give you titles — it gives you tombstones."

She clicked her pen. "So who killed him?"

Ermi's eye twitched. He took another long drag.

"That's the thing about legends. The ending's always blurry. Could've been the Turks. Could've been his own. Could've been the police. Could've been a message from someone bigger. Or maybe he just slipped."

"He slipped?"

"Onto the wrong blade."

She stared.

He smiled thinly.

"You wanted truth. I'm giving you folklore."

Maya tapped the mic. "Off the record?"

He waved a hand.

She turned it off.

"What do you think they're trying to do?"

"The boys?"

She nodded.

"They're building a movie with no ending. And they're casting themselves as the anti-heroes before the climax is written. They think if they look sharp enough, sound scary enough, the ending'll write itself."

"You don't think it'll work?"

Ermi looked at the birds.

"I think even ghosts get shot."

Maya stood, packed up slowly.

He said, just as she reached the door:

"You wanna know what really broke Ade?"

She turned.

"It wasn't prison. It wasn't the war. It was what came after. Watching the city forget."

She said nothing.

"And Kris," he added, "he just wants to be remembered. Even if it kills him."

Maya stepped outside.

The cold slapped her instantly — biting, sour with exhaust.

She turned left down the alley, toward the bus stop.

Didn't notice the figure watching from across the street. Still. Arms folded. No phone. Just eyes.

Eyes that had already decided how this story ends.

The club was called NOIR — of course it was. All black everything. Matte walls. One red light behind the bar that made everyone's face look like a crime scene. The air smelled like designer sweat and melted vape cartridges.

Maya stepped past the rope without showing ID. Kris had put her name on the list, and the bouncer just nodded like he'd been briefed to let ghosts in.

Inside: noise. Pulsing, weaponised bass. Bottles glowing in ice buckets. Girls in streetwear two sizes too small. Boys in jackets too expensive for anyone with legal income. Cameras everywhere — handhelds, phones, mounted ring lights. Flash. Flash. Flash.

At the back, on a raised platform flanked by two men who looked like extras from Top Boy, stood Kris.

Arms wide. Hood off. Pose deliberate.

He wore a Brutalist hoodie — custom, black-on-black embossing. Subtle. Pricey. He grinned like a man who'd already read tomorrow's headlines.

When he spotted Maya, his face lit up even more.

He pushed through the small crowd and met her halfway.

"You made it," he said, already leaning in to kiss her cheek.

She let him.

He smelled like sweat, expensive aftershave, and adrenaline.

"What is this?" she asked.

"Image farming," he said. "Every shot tonight — free marketing. Watch this."

He snapped his fingers at one of the ring light girls.

"Yo, get us."

The girl turned. Posed. Clicked.

Flash. Now Maya was in the frame, too.

"You're using me for PR?" she asked.

Kris winked. "Only if you look good."

She gave a dry smile. "Don't mistake access for permission."

Kris didn't hear her. Or he didn't care. He'd already turned, was already leading her toward the booth, saying something about new music, a collab, a grime artist who might want to use her voiceover in a hook.

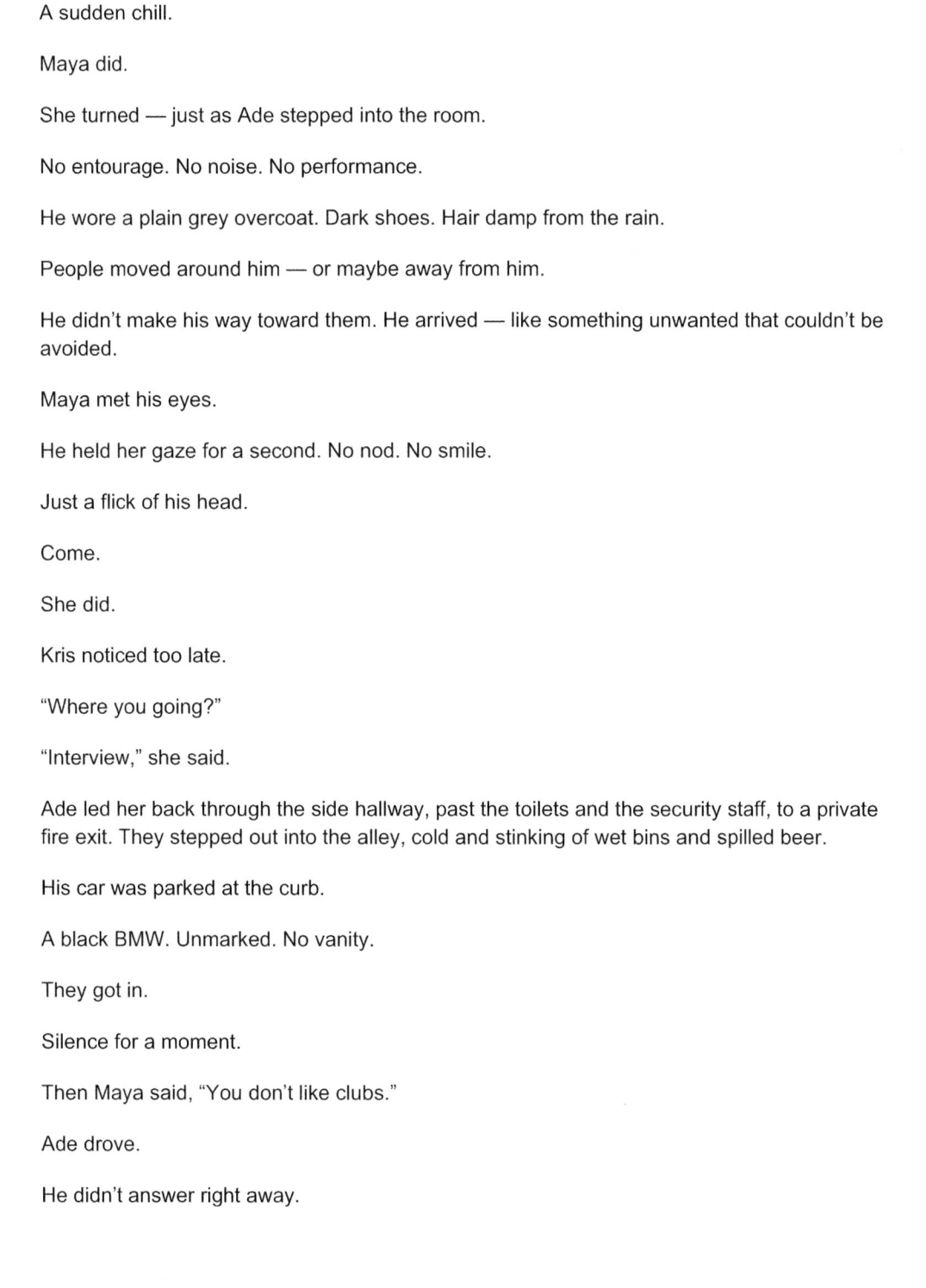

She followed. For now.

He didn't notice the change in air until it hit.

A sudden chill.

Maya did.

She turned — just as Ade stepped into the room.

No entourage. No noise. No performance.

He wore a plain grey overcoat. Dark shoes. Hair damp from the rain.

People moved around him — or maybe away from him.

He didn't make his way toward them. He arrived — like something unwanted that couldn't be avoided.

Maya met his eyes.

He held her gaze for a second. No nod. No smile.

Just a flick of his head.

Come.

She did.

Kris noticed too late.

"Where you going?"

"Interview," she said.

Ade led her back through the side hallway, past the toilets and the security staff, to a private fire exit. They stepped out into the alley, cold and stinking of wet bins and spilled beer.

His car was parked at the curb.

A black BMW. Unmarked. No vanity.

They got in.

Silence for a moment.

Then Maya said, "You don't like clubs."

Ade drove.

He didn't answer right away.

"You don't like being recorded," she added.

Still silence.

Then, flat:

"You keep quoting me."

"I'm quoting what you said."

"I didn't say it to be remembered."

She glanced at him. "Then why say anything at all?"

He didn't answer.

They passed a row of shuttered shops, ghost signs, and kebab wrappers rolling in the wind.

He finally said, "You like knives?"

"Is that a question or a threat?"

"It's a metaphor."

She raised an eyebrow.

"A knife's only useful if it's sharp," he said. "But if you don't sheath it after use, eventually it cuts you back."

"I'm not sure that's how knives work."

"I'm not sure that's how stories work."

He pulled to a stop outside her building. Rain tapped on the windscreen like it had something to say.

"You're making something," he said, eyes forward. "Make sure it's not your own ending."

She studied him.

"You're worried I'll die because I tell your story?"

He looked at her now. Finally. Fully.

"No," he said. "I'm worried you'll think it's yours."

She opened the door.

Paused.

"You want me to stop?"

He said nothing.

She stepped out.

Closed the door.

Didn't look back.

The screen glowed in the dark like a window she couldn't quite close.

Maya sat cross-legged on her floor, headphones in, eyes bloodshot. Her apartment smelled like burnt toast and stubborn thoughts. A near-empty glass of red wine tilted precariously beside her laptop. On the screen: her editing software — full timeline view.

EP1: THE BRUTALISTS – FINAL CUT

Runtime: 28 minutes, 19 seconds.

She'd been through it six times already.

She kept hovering over one clip. A line from Ade — just seven seconds long. Caught offhand in the car, mic still rolling. Not exactly consented to, not exactly off the record either.

"You keep quoting me."

"I didn't say it to be remembered."

The way he'd said it — quiet, low, but sharp. Like it had already been chiseled in stone before she'd hit record.

Maya had clipped it neatly. It landed perfectly at the end of the episode — a punchline, a pause, a warning. It gave everything before it more weight.

She sat back.

Hovered her finger over the delete key.

Paused.

Then dragged it back in.

Click. Lock. Save.

She hit "EXPORT."

Watched the progress bar crawl across the screen.

Then she opened her publishing platform.

Typed a caption:

Episode One: The Brutalists

Two brothers. One city. One myth in the making.

What happens when fear learns to speak?

She clicked "Publish."

The blue loading ring spun once. Twice.

Then: LIVE.

She didn't breathe for the first five minutes.

Then: comments. Notifications. Retweets. DMs.

She watched the numbers jump. 127 listeners. 380. 700. Climbing.

The hashtag #TheBrutalists hit trending within forty-two minutes.

Someone screen-recorded the raid footage and overlaid her voice.

Someone else made a TikTok slideshow of Ade's mugshot and Maya's quote: "He didn't say it to be remembered."

She closed her laptop and poured the rest of the wine.

Across the city, in the brutalist block with flaking paint and boarded stairwells, Ade sat alone on the couch, staring at a borrowed phone.

The podcast played through a speaker someone had left on the table. The sound was tinny but clear. His own voice at the end — ghostlike.

"I didn't say it to be remembered."

He didn't flinch.

Didn't blink.

Just listened.

Outside the window, sirens screamed past without stopping.

He reached forward, clicked the speaker off, and sat in the dark.

Chapter 4 - property and power

The model flat smelled like ambition and lemon polish.

Tall windows looked out over a half-finished courtyard full of scaffolding and discarded hard hats. Inside: cream walls, clean lines, fake designer furniture. A champagne tray on the breakfast island. A projector quietly looped a 3D rendering of "The EastRise Vision" — luxury flats with fake kids, rooftop gardens, and a drone shot of London that didn't include any actual Londoners.

Ade stood near the window, arms crossed, watching a workman smoke below next to a skip.

Kris was all smiles. He floated between two sharp-suited men and a girl in a puffer vest with a perfect camera smile and unreadable accent. Everyone looked like they'd just finished filming an advert for vitamins.

"You see what I mean?" Kris said, half to Ade, half to the room. "This ain't gentrification. It's reclamation. We're the roots. This is us building up, not selling out."

The older developer — Rhys, slick hair, double-breasted jacket, too-white teeth — stepped forward.

"The way we see it, your… profile — it gives us authenticity," he said. "You're not just investing money. You're investing story. Local colour. Myth."

"Heritage," added the girl, smiling. "Real London energy."

Ade blinked.

"Real London energy," he repeated. "You say that in Chelsea too?"

They laughed. Kris didn't.

Ade turned slightly toward Kris. "Who's paying for the permits?"

Rhys's smile flickered — then bounced back. "That's covered. We've got a shell on the books — KLL Holdings. They handle the paperwork, we handle the press. You just… keep the name hot."

Ade's eyes narrowed. "KLL. What's that stand for?"

"Nothing," said Rhys too quickly.

"Everything," said the girl at the same time.

Ade clocked both answers.

He turned to Kris. "You read the contracts?"

"They're sending them tonight."

"They bring a lawyer?"

"They're lawyers."

Ade didn't respond.

Instead, he walked over to the projector, stared at the looping video. In one shot, a drone flew across the Thames and over glittering towers that didn't exist yet. Then cut to a crowd of models laughing on a rooftop bar that had clearly been photoshopped.

"Where's the community centre?" he asked.

The room quieted.

"What?"

"In the render. Where's the flats for the families already here? Where's the park for the kids? Where's the block with the rust stains and the chip shop downstairs? You building over that?"

Rhys cleared his throat. "This isn't… that kind of project."

"No," Ade said. "It's not."

Kris stepped forward, trying to soften it.

"Ade—"

But Ade was already heading for the door.

He paused in the threshold.

"You want the name," he said. "Fine. But names come with history. You pave over that, it doesn't go away. It waits. Under the concrete."

The girl smiled too politely. "That's very poetic."

Ade stared at her.

"No. That's very real."

He walked out without waiting for Kris.

Outside, the wind smelled of cement and cold ambition. Workers hauled steel beams while someone shouted over a walkie. Ade stood under the half-formed archway of what would someday be a glass tower — if no one burned it down first.

Kris caught up a minute later, breathless.

"You could've chilled," he said. "That was networking."

"No," Ade said. "That was bait."

"They're giving us a chance to play big."

"They're giving us a paper leash."

Kris ran a hand through his hair.

"I'm trying to build something. Not just take corners and film it. You said legacy. This is legacy."

Ade turned to him. Eyes hard. Cold.

"Legacy is what people say after you're dead. Right now, all we've got is debt. And I'm not owing suits who smile that much."

Kris didn't reply.

Ade walked to the car. Slammed the door harder than he needed to.

The towers above them kept climbing — empty shells waiting to be filled with ghosts.

The gym smelled like mildew and ghosts.

Maya stepped inside behind Kris, the heavy door creaking back into place behind them. The floorboards moaned under her boots. Dust swirled in the sunlight slanting through a crack in the ceiling. Old gloves hung from hooks on the wall, limp as dead hands. A torn Everlast bag drooped in the corner, leaking sand.

Kris spread his arms wide like he was unveiling a penthouse.

"Picture it," he said. "Ring in the middle. Ropes bright red. Spotlights. DJ booth where that mold patch is. Bag work down the back. Weight benches over here. Upstairs, a little café — smoothies, Turkish coffee, kombucha. Health meets heritage."

Maya scanned the room, holding her phone low, recording ambient noise: the creak of rope, the occasional drop of water echoing somewhere deep in the walls.

"Sounds expensive," she said.

Kris grinned. "Don't worry. It's covered."

"By who?"

"Investors."

She stopped walking.

"Kris."

He turned, still smiling, but something about it was off. Tight at the edges.

"Relax," he said. "It's clean. The place is under a trust, old community grant — legit on paper. All I've gotta do is make it look like it's lifting the area."

"And in the meantime?"

"In the meantime, it's where money goes to breathe. Before it goes out again wearing a suit."

Maya nodded slowly, walking toward a crumbling locker. She opened it. Found nothing but dust and a cracked photo of a kid in gloves — maybe ten years old. Maybe younger.

"You're laundering," she said flatly.

Kris winked. "I'm rebranding."

She leaned against the lockers, arms crossed. "And Ade's cool with all this?"

Kris hesitated — just for a second.

"Course."

"You tell him where the money's coming from?"

The smile faltered.

"Why wouldn't I?"

"Kris."

He exhaled, looked away. "It's politics. It's not a big deal."

"What politics?"

"Some of Lenny's guys. Old connections. Mutual interest."

Maya stared. "You're taking money from Lenny Uzun."

"Not directly."

"You're laundering Uzun's cash through a boxing gym in your brother's name?"

"Not in his name," Kris snapped. "Just… under the umbrella. Look — he's too busy watching shadows to build anything real. Someone's gotta play chess."

Maya didn't speak. The air between them stretched thin.

Kris stepped closer.

"Don't put this in your episode," he said.

"I haven't even turned on the mic yet."

"Still. Off the record."

"Only if you give me something real in return."

He laughed, but there was no weight in it.

"You're scary when you're like this."

"No," she said. "I'm honest. Which makes me rare in this building."

Kris didn't respond.

She hit record anyway — silently. Just ambient sound again.

The ropes creaked above. Dust settled like it had just heard a secret.

The tower block leaned slightly left, like it had started giving up on standing sometime in the nineties. Broken buzzers. Windows fogged with grime. A plastic bag drifted lazily in the stairwell draft, looping over itself like it was trying to escape.

Ade climbed the steps alone.

He never trusted lifts.

Flat 17C. The door was new — too new. White, metal, no scratches. Clean edges. It didn't match anything around it. He knocked once, hard.

It opened halfway. A chain rattled inside.

"Marku?" the voice asked — nasal, wary, the sound of someone who rarely left his laptop.

"Yeah," Ade said.

The door closed. A few seconds passed. Then reopened — this time fully.

The man inside wore a pressed polo shirt tucked into joggers and a sheen of stress sweat. Late fifties, balding. His glasses were fogged from breathing too fast. The flat behind him was clinical — laminate flooring, no furniture except a desk stacked with property folders and a legal pad with someone's name half-scribbled out.

"Come in," he said, stepping aside. "Please."

Ade didn't thank him. Just walked in.

"Tea?" the man asked, already knowing the answer.

"No."

They sat at the desk. The landlord cleared his throat like it would buy him confidence.

"The paperwork's ready. It's an open lease, nothing complicated — the original tenant association collapsed back in 2009. It's just been used for storage since then."

"And it's yours to move," Ade said.

The man nodded. "Technically. On paper."

"Then move it."

The man hesitated. "You… understand this won't be registered through the council."

"I understand perfectly."

"And that this property is marked for potential demolition in the next eighteen months?"

Ade leaned forward. "Then you'll get your money now, before the bulldozers come. Or don't — and this whole block stays haunted by your indecision."

The landlord swallowed hard.

He opened a drawer, slid a folded contract across the desk. Already filled out. Already signed — just waiting for one more name.

Ade glanced at it. Didn't read the fine print. Pulled a pen from his coat. Wrote only a single word: RIGOR.

Not his name. Not anyone's. Just enough.

The man tucked it away, cleared his throat again. "And the payment?"

"Tomorrow. Cash."

"I'll need a drop location."

"You'll get one. Use a fresh burner phone. Smash it after."

The landlord nodded.

Ade stood.

"Anything else?" he asked.

"No," the man said, too quickly. "No."

An hour later, in a fluorescent-lit office buried behind a sandwich shop police front, Detective Cal Lowry stared at the unsigned lease agreement and the shaky voice memo that came with it.

The landlord's voice buzzed through tinny speakers:

"…I didn't want to call this in, but he scared me. Something about the way he said 'cash.' No receipts. No council forms. It's gangland, I'm sure of it. He signed with a fake name. I recorded this in case I go missing…"

Lowry leaned back in his chair, let the smoke from his cigarette rise like slow accusation.

He tapped his pen against the desk once. Twice.

Then he circled the name at the top of the file:

PROPERTY: 17C MARSHALL COURT

SIGNATORY: "RIGOR"

He smiled.

"Finally," he muttered. "A goddamn thread."

The video arrived with no subject line.

Just a WeTransfer link, dumped in Maya's burner inbox — the account she only checked when she was chasing threats or lies.

She stared at it over her second coffee of the day, hesitated for a moment, then clicked.

Grainy CCTV footage. No sound. A nightclub — dark, moody, somewhere expensive. Timestamped two weeks ago. The angle was overhead, high and dirty. Maya recognized the layout. NOIR. The same night she'd left early with Ade.

Two figures at a corner table.

Kris Marku.

Lenny Uzun.

Handshake.

Not businesslike. Familiar. Grinning.

Kris leaned in. Said something. Lenny nodded.

Money changed hands. A briefcase. No reaction from the bouncers.

Maya paused it.

Zoomed.

No mistaking it.

She stared at the screen, heart beginning to race. There was no audio, but she could feel the conversation. No tension. No bluffing. Just two men who'd already done this before.

She grabbed her coat and her recorder.

The gym was quiet, but the lights were on. Inside, Kris was alone, pacing. His hoodie was off, and his eyes were darker than usual — sunken, twitchy at the edges. The sound of his footsteps on the wooden floor echoed like a metronome for bad decisions.

He barely looked up when she entered.

"You here for the episode?" he asked. "Not a great day."

She held up her phone. Hit play.

The video looped.

His face froze.

He watched it in full, once. Then again.

Then he chuckled, low and dry.

"Shit travels fast."

"You didn't deny it."

"Should I?"

"You said it was politics," Maya said. "You told me you weren't involved."

"I said it wasn't direct. Still isn't."

"Don't lie to me, Kris."

He stepped closer, smile thinning.

"Why are you so angry?"

"Because I put your voice in my show. I let you shape the narrative. And you left this out."

"I left a lot out," he said. "So did you."

She blinked.

"What's that supposed to mean?"

"You know Ade would've walked the moment he saw that briefcase," Kris said. "You know he still thinks we can scare our way into legitimacy. But this?" He tapped the phone. "This is how things move."

"It's betrayal."

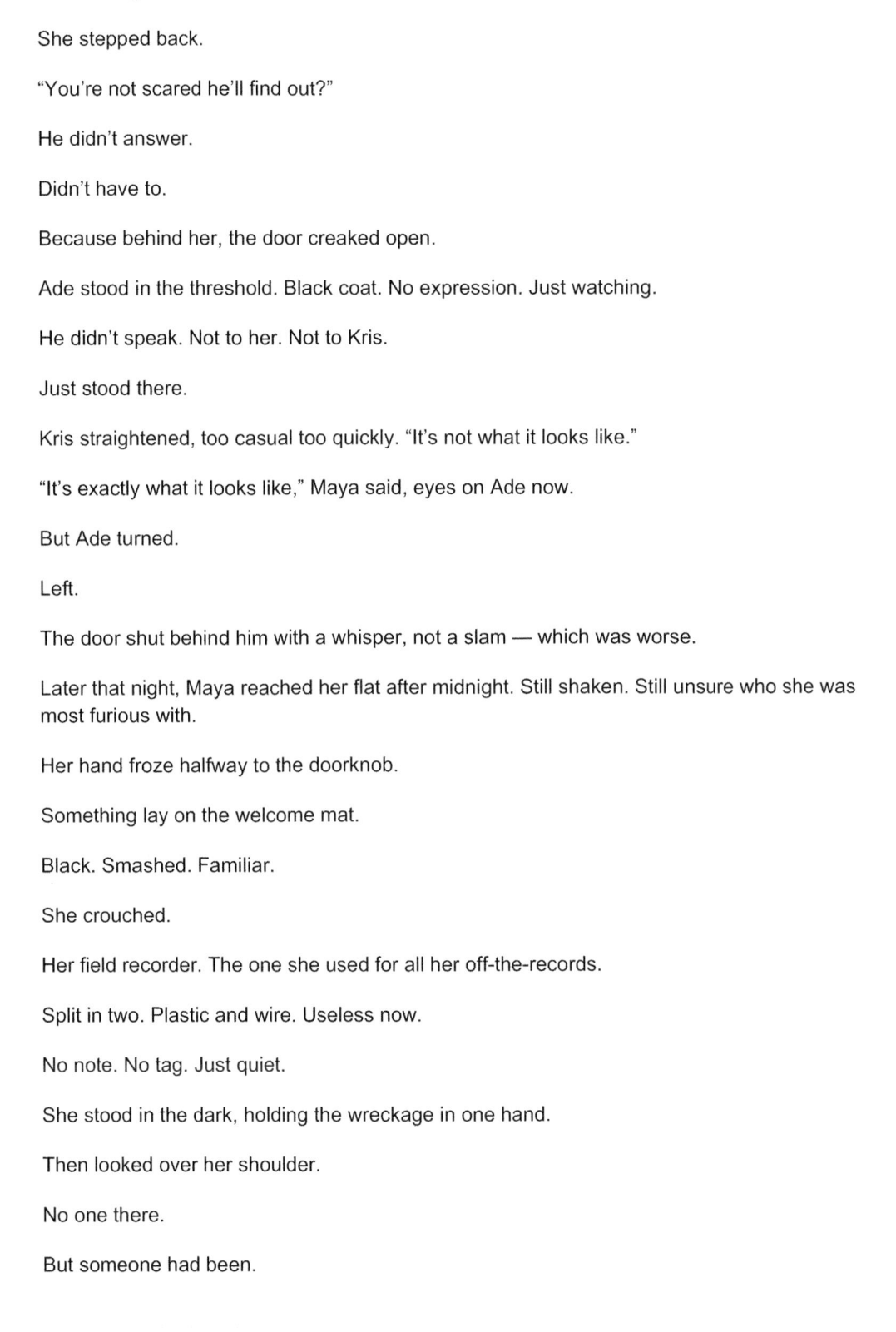

"It's leverage."

She stepped back.

"You're not scared he'll find out?"

He didn't answer.

Didn't have to.

Because behind her, the door creaked open.

Ade stood in the threshold. Black coat. No expression. Just watching.

He didn't speak. Not to her. Not to Kris.

Just stood there.

Kris straightened, too casual too quickly. "It's not what it looks like."

"It's exactly what it looks like," Maya said, eyes on Ade now.

But Ade turned.

Left.

The door shut behind him with a whisper, not a slam — which was worse.

Later that night, Maya reached her flat after midnight. Still shaken. Still unsure who she was most furious with.

Her hand froze halfway to the doorknob.

Something lay on the welcome mat.

Black. Smashed. Familiar.

She crouched.

Her field recorder. The one she used for all her off-the-records.

Split in two. Plastic and wire. Useless now.

No note. No tag. Just quiet.

She stood in the dark, holding the wreckage in one hand.

Then looked over her shoulder.

No one there.

But someone had been.

Lowry sat in a transit van disguised as a disused plumber's truck, biting a pen that tasted like chemicals and old breath. Rain tapped the roof like impatient fingers. Beside him, his tech officer — bored, bearded, young enough to think crime was content — monitored three screens and a tangle of microphones wired into a flat down the street.

The feed was choppy but usable.

"Boxing gym's active again," the tech said. "They've got new gear in there. Some of it still has the tags on."

Lowry sipped cold coffee and said nothing.

"You know we're two steps from a warrant," the tech offered.

Lowry stared at the screen. Ade Marku walked into frame.

Alone.

Dark coat. No umbrella. No words. Just quiet tension pressed into human shape.

Lowry leaned forward. "Turn it up."

Inside the gym, the air was thick with damp and dust. Ade moved through the space like it belonged to someone else. The walls were newly scrubbed, but the floor still bore the scuff marks of past violence. He stepped over a half-unpacked delivery box filled with cheap gloves.

The lights flickered.

Something buzzed in the distance — a faulty sensor or a lazy spirit.

Then: a sound.

Low. Muffled.

He followed it.

Down the corridor, past the office, through the changing rooms. A door ajar. Locker room.

On the tiled floor: a boy.

Thin. Twitching. Maybe sixteen. Face pale, lips tinged purple. A foil square on the bench beside him, blackened at the edges.

A needle on the floor. Half full.

Ade didn't blink. Didn't panic.

He dropped to one knee, checked the pulse.

Still there — just barely.

He lifted the boy like he weighed nothing, carried him out with a kind of practiced grace. Like this wasn't the first time.

Out the back exit. Into the alley.

He didn't call for help. Didn't shout. Just propped the kid upright against the wall, opened his airway, and waited — face blank, eyes scanning the dark like he expected someone to try and take the moment away.

In the van, Lowry watched it unfold in silence.

The tech murmured, "You want me to tag that?"

Lowry nodded slowly.

"That's our crack. He's doing clean-up. That means there's dirt."

He lit a cigarette, hands steady now.

"Pull the footage. Cut everything else. Just him. The kid. And the cleanup."

"Should I watermark it?"

"No."

"Who's it for?"

Lowry exhaled smoke.

"Someone who doesn't need to ask."

The file transferred. Fast. Quiet.

No label. Just a timestamp and an image:

ADE_MARKU_23:41

Across the city, a screen pinged in a dark room.

No police lights. No sirens. Just someone watching — and deciding.

Chapter 5 - Clout and Consequences

The warehouse was condemned in 2007. It still looked surprised to be standing.

Kris had picked it for the atmosphere — rusted scaffolding, broken skylights, oil stains older than the kids bouncing in the queue. No working toilets. No permits. But it had space. And more importantly: signal.

The entrance was marked by a red flare stuck in a shopping trolley. A masked teen with a barcode tattoo on his neck waved people through one at a time, checking their phone screens for the private livestream code. Anyone filming inside without permission had their phone tossed in a steel bucket.

Kris stood just inside the ring of portable floodlights, flanked by two tall, silent lads in all black. One of them carried a first-aid kit. The other carried a pipe wrapped in tape.

Maya arrived with her press lanyard tucked under a coat that didn't look warm enough. She pushed through the crowd — influencers in Balenciaga knockoffs, grime artists drinking straight from the bottle, two kids she recognized from viral shoplifting videos.

The center of the warehouse had been cleared and roped off into a ring. Makeshift bleachers — pallets stacked on tires — rose around it. A live feed camera was rigged to a drone above. Every so often, it buzzed closer to the action, tilting down like it was hungry.

Kris caught Maya's eye.

He winked.

She did not wink back.

The first bout was a blur — bare-knuckle, fast, brutal. A crowd favorite in a tiger mask versus a skinny kid with no rhythm but plenty of rage. The kid won. Cheers erupted. Camera flashes painted sweat silver.

By the third fight, Maya had already recorded ten solid minutes of audio: crowd reactions, punch sounds, Kris giving pre-fight interviews about "urban reclamation through sanctioned aggression."

Her phone buzzed once.

Anonymous message.

Just an address.

Lenny's office.

She ignored it.

The final fight was scheduled for midnight. Two undefeateds. One local. One outsider brought in by Kris for "shock value." No names. Just masks and stats.

Kris stepped into the ring before the bell.

"Before we go," he said into the mic, "just remember — this ain't sport. This is culture. And culture don't apologize."

The crowd roared.

Ade wasn't there.

Maya kept looking over her shoulder. But nothing. No shadow. No presence.

The fighters circled. Cameras up. Drone tilting down.

Then the bell rang.

It was less a fight, more a ritual.

First few blows were cautious. Then came the flurry — elbows, knees, palms slapping flesh. The local boy slipped once — then recovered. The outsider ducked. Countered. They both bled early. Cheered for it.

Then something changed.

A shape in the local fighter's hand.

Flash of silver.

Too fast.

Too late.

A gasp — not from the crowd, but from the ring.

Blood. Real blood. Too much, too fast.

The outsider dropped. Not theatrical. Not sportsmanlike. Dropped.

Chaos fractured the silence.

Screams. Phones pulled. Half the crowd surged forward. The other half surged back. Someone yelled for medics — there were none. The kid with the first-aid kit froze.

Kris vaulted into the ring.

"Get back!" he shouted. "No cameras!"

Too late.

The drone kept hovering. Still live.

Maya stood frozen as someone stumbled past her, face pale, shoes red.

The music never stopped. It just felt like it had.

In the ring, Kris tried to press a towel against the wound. His face — still performing. Still clenching for control.

It wasn't working.

The boy convulsed.

And the feed went viral.

By the time the police arrived, the crowd was already gone — dispersed like smoke, filtered into side streets, back alleys, ride shares. The only things left were blood on the ring ropes and a pile of crushed vape pens near the exit.

The body was covered with a silver tarp. The fighter's mask still on. Just a red puddle creeping from beneath, like the floor had started drinking.

Outside, blue lights flashed against the warehouse's rusted walls. No sirens now. Just flashing proof of how late law always was.

Kris sat on the back bumper of a delivery van, hoodie off, hands shaking. Two burner phones beside him. One cracked. One ringing. He didn't answer either.

Maya stood ten feet away, watching.

She didn't record.

Not this.

Inside, the officers were taking statements from security who didn't exist. Asking for permits that weren't printed. Scribbling names that meant nothing. No one said Kris. No one said Marku. But it was already too late.

The footage had been clipped. Edited. Reuploaded.

The hashtags were multiplying like bruises:

#FightNightMurder

#EastEndCarnage

#TheBrutalists

An hour later, in Ermi's flat, Ade stood in the middle of the room, fists clenched so tight his knuckles had gone white again.

Kris walked in slow.

Didn't sit.

Didn't speak.

Just waited.

"What the f— was that?" Ade said. Quiet. Flat. Like a razor laid on a counter.

Kris shrugged. "It went wrong."

"Went wrong?"

"He wasn't supposed to have a blade—"

"You picked the fighters."

"I picked the venue. The hype. The feed. I didn't pick the murder."

Ade stepped forward.

"No one knew the location. Not even half the crew. So how did Lenny's boy end up in your ring, bleeding out on my f—ing name?"

Kris flinched. "You think I set that up?"

Ade didn't blink. "I think someone did."

"You think it was Maya?"

The question landed like a brick thrown at glass.

Ade said nothing.

Kris took the silence personally.

"Come on, man. She had the audio. She was in the room. Always is. Maybe you trust her too much."

Ade's voice was colder now.

"She doesn't know how to set up a murder. You do."

Kris laughed, but there was no humor left in it. "You think I wanted that kid to die? That's not good for the brand, bro. That's not content. That's closure."

Ade walked past him.

Stopped at the door.

"You're not building anything," he said. "You're filming the demolition."

And then he left.

Back at the gym, the lights were off. The doors were locked. But someone had already tagged the shutter with red spray paint.

One word:

PAYBACK.

The interviewer was twenty-one, wore sunglasses indoors, and said "vibe check" without irony.

They met in a studio with white curtains and hanging plants, somewhere in Hackney Wick where the rent was subsidized by ego. Kris sat across from her, legs wide, hoodie crisp, jaw sharp. Behind him, a neon sign read: "MAKE IT MAKE SENSE."

She smiled with shark-like softness. The camera blinked red.

"Okay," she said. "So — let's address the blood."

Kris smiled back. Perfectly timed.

"I didn't throw a punch," he said. "But I built the ring. That's true."

She raised an eyebrow. "You feel responsible?"

"I feel like responsibility's a privilege when you get to rewrite the story. Which I do."

"So you're saying this is about narrative control?"

"I'm saying if people want myth, they better pay for the ink."

Behind the scenes, the producers nodded like they were watching a prophet.

Maya watched the clip on her phone in silence. From her desk. From her own studio. Her tea had gone cold. Again.

She clicked pause right as Kris gave his signature half-smile.

The one he used before he said something reckless.

Later, she found him in a back corner of a café in Bethnal Green, tucked behind two bodyguards who kept scanning for imaginary snipers.

She didn't sit.

"You're building a house out of dry leaves," she said.

Kris looked up from his phone, barely phased. "Better than waiting in the dark."

"You're not controlling the story. You're feeding it."

"I am the story."

Maya leaned in.

"You're not a legend, Kris. You're a warning."

Across town, Ade sat on the floor of Ermi's flat, back against the wall, eating cold soup straight from the can. Ermi sat in his chair, feet up, pigeons shifting in their cages. The news played low on the TV — another clip of the fight. The body blurred, but the mood unmistakable.

Ermi didn't speak for a while.

Then:

"You know what gets kings killed?"

Ade didn't look up. "Knives. Poison. Ego."

"No," Ermi said. "Loyalty. Given to the wrong son."

Ade kept eating.

"The boy's not evil," Ermi added. "He's hungry. But hunger turns dangerous when it starts chewing its own tongue."

Ade set the can down. Wiped his mouth with his sleeve.

"He's not ready."

"He's already acting like he's crowned."

Ermi pulled something from a drawer — an envelope. Fat. Unmarked.

"Heard from Lenny's people," he said. "They want a sit-down. One-on-one. Not Kris. You."

Ade stared at the envelope.

Ermi tapped it. "He's not threatening. Yet. But this ain't a warning. This is a window. You know what that means."

Ade didn't speak.

But he didn't refuse it either.

Ermi stood. Lit a cigarette. Watched it burn.

"Choose what kind of brother you want to be," he said. "Before someone else chooses for you."

That night, Kris posted another clip.

Fifty seconds of edited drone footage. Fight night highlights. Masked fighters. Cheers. Soundtrack: something bass-heavy and theatrical. Over it, his voice:

"They write about us like we're villains. Fine. But remember this — villains get remembered."

The comments were split.

The shares were not.

The clip was only thirteen seconds long.

But it hit like a bullet to the brand.

No music. No voiceover. Just raw, handheld footage — not from the drone, not from the official feed. This was ground-level. Dirty. Real. A side angle no one knew existed.

The camera caught it perfectly:

The moment the body hit the floor.

The way Kris smiled — not wide, not exaggerated, just enough.

And in the background, the twitching legs.

Then: a towel tossed. A hand over a lens. Cut to black.

No caption. Just a title:

"This your king?"

It spread fast.

First TikTok. Then Twitter. Then Reddit. The forums. The underground threads. People paused it. Zoomed it. Picked it apart frame by frame like it was a Zapruder film.

Kris Marku mid-grin.

Blood on his shoes.

Blurred face, but unmistakable.

Sponsors ghosted them overnight.

A local rap label deleted a collab post.

One of Kris's burner merch accounts was reported and taken down.

Maya woke up to thirty-seven notifications.

She scrolled through her mentions.

Someone had screen-capped the clip and tagged her directly.

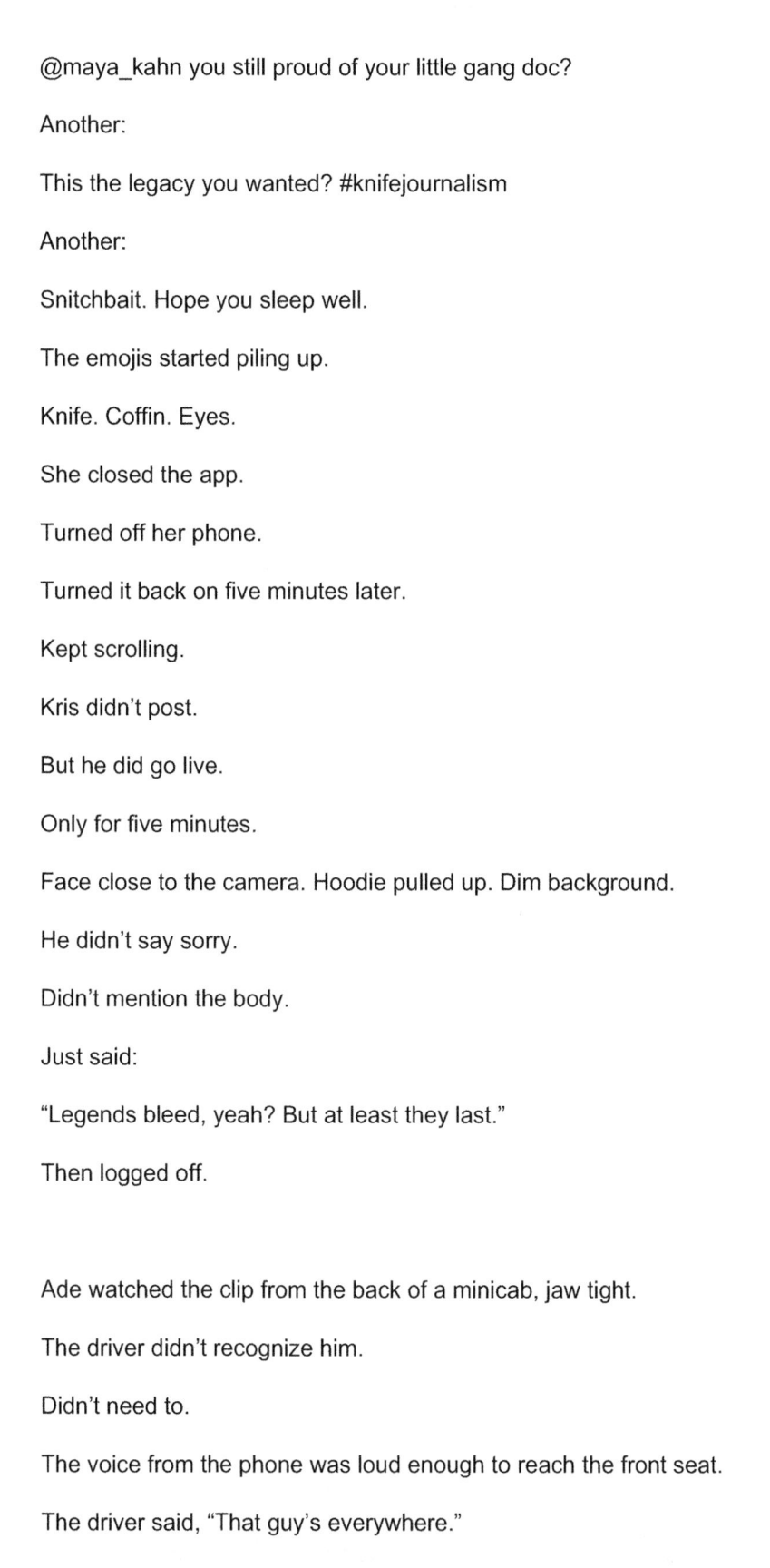

@maya_kahn you still proud of your little gang doc?

Another:

This the legacy you wanted? #knifejournalism

Another:

Snitchbait. Hope you sleep well.

The emojis started piling up.

Knife. Coffin. Eyes.

She closed the app.

Turned off her phone.

Turned it back on five minutes later.

Kept scrolling.

Kris didn't post.

But he did go live.

Only for five minutes.

Face close to the camera. Hoodie pulled up. Dim background.

He didn't say sorry.

Didn't mention the body.

Just said:

"Legends bleed, yeah? But at least they last."

Then logged off.

Ade watched the clip from the back of a minicab, jaw tight.

The driver didn't recognize him.

Didn't need to.

The voice from the phone was loud enough to reach the front seat.

The driver said, "That guy's everywhere."

Ade didn't respond.

He just closed the app, pocketed the phone, and stared out the window.

⸺

Across town, Lenny Uzun stood in a glass office overlooking the Thames.

The footage played on mute.

His expression didn't change.

But he nodded once.

Someone behind him said, "We move now?"

Lenny said nothing.

Then: "Wait. Let him come."

The countdown hit zero.

LIVE: 00:00:00

"Brutalist Response — Kris Marku"

Fifteen thousand viewers and climbing.

Kris sat on a low stool in the center of the gym, a Brutalist banner draped behind him like a war flag. The lighting was deliberate — harsh shadows, bright eyes. Just enough menace to be iconic.

He wasn't dressed for apology.

Grey joggers, black hoodie, chain tucked in. Not a crease in sight.

No script. No handlers. No Ade.

He looked directly at the camera.

"Let me make this real clear," he said. "I don't run. I don't lie. I build. You lot wanna paint me as a villain? Fine. I'll frame the picture myself."

The comments flashed like bullets:

" GOAT."

"Ain't even sweating."

"Wait where's Ade?"

"He smiling again???"

"This ain't a press conference, it's a funeral."

Kris kept going.

"They want us gone. That means we matter. If they ain't writing you into the history books, write your own f—ing book."

He paused, leaned forward.

"And no — I'm not sorry."

Then he killed the stream.

Ade wasn't watching.

He was sitting in a sterile office across from Lenny Uzun, both hands folded calmly in front of him. A single light buzzed overhead. No guards. No desk between them. Just space and consequence.

Lenny poured tea from a Turkish pot. Didn't offer any.

He didn't look angry.

Just done.

"You know what I hate?" Lenny said, stirring. "Not betrayal. Not theft. Not even blood. I hate amateurs. People who think clout is a shield. It's not. It's a f—ing beacon."

Ade said nothing.

Lenny sipped.

"Your brother cost me more than a name. He cost me silence. And now people are watching. When people watch, they expect a response."

He leaned back.

"So. Here's what I'm offering: you step out. Step away. Cut him loose — publicly, privately, doesn't matter. You disappear, and I forget your surname."

He tapped a finger against the desk.

"You stay? You burn with him."

Silence.

Ade's jaw clenched. Just slightly.

Lenny watched him carefully, like a man watching a knife decide which way to fall.

"Well?"

Ade stood.

Didn't answer.

Didn't shake.

Didn't nod.

Just walked out.

⸱

Kris's phone buzzed.

No new viewers.

No likes.

Just a single message. From Ade.

We need to talk. Not here. Roof. Tonight.

Chapter 6 - Brothers Debt

The rooftop was cold and quiet — the kind of quiet that felt personal.

The estate sprawled below like a broken chessboard. Floodlights from the nearby yard flickered against satellite dishes and flapping tarps. In the distance, the Shard blinked like a threat. Up here, it felt like London had forgotten to breathe.

Kris was already waiting — leaning on the ledge, hoodie up, shoulders tense. He didn't turn when Ade stepped out of the stairwell. Didn't speak either. Just kept looking out over the city like it might blink first.

Ade walked slowly. Hands in coat pockets.

"I came alone," he said.

"Yeah," Kris replied. "You always do."

They stood a few feet apart, not looking at each other.

For a second, it was like they were kids again. Same roof. Same view. Different war.

"You watched the stream?" Kris asked.

"No."

"You saw the clip?"

"I saw the blood."

Kris exhaled sharply through his nose. "That's not on me."

"You picked the venue. You picked the feed. You smiled."

"You think I meant it?"

"I don't care if you meant it."

Kris turned finally. Eyes dark, lined.

"You came up here to tell me what? That you're done?"

"No," Ade said. "I came to tell you I can still fix this. But not with you smiling over corpses."

Kris stepped in. "You think I planned that?"

"I think you let it happen."

"I think you're jealous," Kris said. "Because I made something. I made people look. I made people care. You're just a shadow in the back."

Ade's jaw didn't move, but something in his eyes snapped — quiet and sharp.

"You think being looked at is the same as being followed?"

Kris laughed. "You sound like Ermi."

"Ermi knows when a knife's close."

"What are you gonna do?" Kris said. "Walk away? Again?"

Ade didn't answer.

"Bro," Kris said, softer now, more tired than angry. "You and me. We are the story. No matter how it ends."

Ade stepped closer. For a second, Kris flinched.

"You really want to die on camera?"

Kris didn't reply.

Ade held his stare for a breath, maybe two.

Then turned.

Walked toward the door.

He paused once — hand on the frame.

"Last time I leave this roof," he said. "Next time I come up here, it's for the view."

Then he was gone.

Kris didn't move for a long time.

The wind picked up, tugging at his hood.

The city didn't blink.

The poker room wasn't a room.

It was a refrigerated garage in the back of a butcher shop, just off the A13 — half-lit, floor slick with old ice and the smell of bleach and meat. Four folding tables. One electric heater. Cigarette smoke curled up toward the cracked ceiling tiles like it wanted to escape first.

Kris walked in with swagger so thick it needed subtitles.

"Bit cold for a game night," he said, tugging his hoodie sleeves up to the elbow. "Could've sent me a nicer invite."

No one laughed.

Five men sat around the table already. None were smiling. One wore gloves. One wore a gold tooth that caught the light like it was part of a trap. The dealer — a boy with tattoos up his throat — nodded for him to sit.

"You're late," he said.

Kris grinned, pulling out the chair. "Style has no schedule."

Chips were stacked. Cards dealt. No introductions. Just clicks and nods and the sound of someone chewing too loudly.

For the first two hands, it felt like a real game.

Then it changed.

The gold-tooth man looked up. "You still filming?"

Kris didn't blink. "Only on days that matter."

"Every day matters," said the one in gloves.

Another hand dealt. Small blind. Raise. Call.

"Word is," someone muttered, "you got a kid killed on camera."

Kris tilted his head. "Wasn't a kid. Was a fighter. Signed up. Took a swing. Took one back."

"No gloves, no medic, no permit," said the tattooed boy. "Sounds like slaughter."

Kris smiled thin. "You gonna play, or just throw shade?"

"We're playing," said gloves.

And that's when the real game began.

The pot grew.

The eyes got quieter.

No one looked at their cards anymore.

It wasn't about winning. It was about positioning.

By the sixth hand, the gold-tooth man tossed his cards without looking.

"We watched the footage," he said. "He wasn't nobody. He was Lenny's blood."

The garage got colder.

Kris didn't move.

"He didn't introduce himself," he said carefully.

"You made him famous," said the dealer. "Now Lenny's got funerals trending."

Gloves reached under the table. Set something down beside the pot.

Not a weapon.

A photograph.

Black-and-white. Old. Folded at the corners.

Kris glanced.

It was a shot of Ermi, younger. Standing beside Valon Marku. Pre-fall. Pre-blood.

The dealer tapped it.

"You're not the first golden boy to think he could outshine his shadow."

Kris's smile died.

"Is this the part where you pull a gun?" he asked.

Gloves shook his head. "Guns are for loud debts. This is quiet. Lenny don't want your apology. He wants your awareness."

"What does that mean?"

"It means you owe," said gold tooth. "And the interest don't come in cash."

⸱

Kris left without speaking.

No winnings. No chips. Just a bruised ego and a growing silence in his chest.

He didn't notice until he got back to his flat that his phone was missing.

Later that night, it turned up in Maya's inbox.

Wrapped in cling film.

No charger.

Just one missed call in the log.

UNKNOWN — 3:13am

The first time she noticed, Maya was leaving her corner shop with oat milk and rolling papers.

A man across the street — not staring. Not obvious. Just lingering. Pretending to argue with his phone while standing completely still. Hoodie pulled up. Face angled away from the light.

The second time, he was behind her on the Victoria line. Too clean. Nothing in his hands. No headphones. No movement, even when the train braked hard enough to throw a kid into a pole.

She didn't confront him.

She just walked faster. Took different turns. Waited to see if it happened again.

It did.

By nightfall, she'd locked every window, taped over the peephole, and buried her best mic behind a stack of unread zines. The red recording light always drew attention.

She pulled her laptop onto her legs, wrapped in two layers of blanket, and opened the archive folder.

> INTERVIEWS > ERMI RAW > 2024_09_16_UNEDITED

Run time: 00:48:22

She hit play.

Ermi's voice filtered in low and tired:

"You think they remember who fired the first shot? No. They remember the one who bled best."

She skipped ahead. Past the long-winded metaphors. Past the cackling pigeons in the background. Until—

Maya (off mic): "You ever talk to Valon about legacy?"

Ermi: "Valon didn't talk. He gave orders."

Maya: "So the stories about the night he died… they're true?"

(Pause)

Ermi: "Some are. But what no one says is — he wasn't killed by a rival. Not really."

Maya: "What do you mean?"

Ermi (quiet): "He walked into that alley thinking his son would follow. But Kris never did."

She paused the file.

Heart kicking in her chest.

Rewound. Played it again.

Same line. Same quiet.

"…Kris never did."

She hadn't used that clip. It was too ambiguous, too speculative. At the time, it hadn't felt usable. But now?

Now someone was following her.

And this — this wasn't a theory.

This was a motive.

⸫

Her phone buzzed.

UNKNOWN NUMBER

One message.

We see what you keep. Delete it.

No name. No threat.

Just clarity.

She turned off the lights.

Then turned the mic back on.

The old school smelled like wet concrete and dried ink.

The kind of building the city didn't bother condemning because it had already erased it from memory. "Temporary closure" said the sign on the gates. Ten years ago.

Now: shattered windows, empty fire extinguishers, desks rusted to the floor. The mural on the west wall still showed cartoon children holding hands under the words BE THE FUTURE. One had a bullet hole through its eye.

Ermi led the way down the hallway with a flashlight gripped like a weapon. Ade followed, silent, hands in coat pockets, boots echoing over broken tiles.

"Caretaker's nephew owns the deed now," Ermi said. "Long-term lease. No council eyes. Plenty of space."

Ade barely glanced around.

"Too exposed."

"That's what you said about the gym," Ermi muttered.

"It was."

They turned a corner into what used to be a library. Light filtered in through cracked skylights. Dust particles floated like ash. Books still lined the shelves — warped, water-damaged, unreadable.

Ermi sat on a teacher's desk that looked like it would snap under him.

"You gonna talk to me?" he asked. "Or are we just playing haunted house today?"

Ade walked the perimeter of the room, tracing his fingers along a peeling map of East London.

"You ever think about leaving?" he asked.

Ermi chuckled. "I've only ever thought about leaving. Just didn't think it'd still look like this."

Ade turned.

"I need to get Kris out."

Ermi raised an eyebrow. "Out of what?"

"The frame. The city. The game."

"You mean exile."

Ade nodded.

Ermi lit a cigarette, watching the smoke coil toward the ceiling.

"You think you can fix this like a chessboard," he said. "Move one piece, box up the rest."

"It's not just about fixing it."

"No," Ermi said. "It's about control. You think silence makes you invisible, but it just makes people fill in the blanks."

Ade said nothing.

"You want my help?" Ermi said. "Then hear this: ghosts don't win. They just linger. You want your brother alive, you better make him believe he's already dead out here."

Ade met his gaze.

"I'm not saving him from Lenny," he said. "I'm saving him from himself."

Ermi tapped ash off the edge of the desk.

"Then you better start quick."

Outside, a black car idled at the edge of the school's ruined car park.

Inside it, two figures sat watching the exit.

One held a tablet.

On the screen: Maya's face. Frozen mid-sentence.

And the waveform of a voice about to shake everything.

The clip dropped at 4:00 a.m.

No tag. No watermark. No intro music. Just a waveform. A black screen. A caption:

"The real reason Valon Marku died."

The audio started low, like breath fogging glass.

ERMI (voice only):

"Valon was a lot of things. But careful? Nah. He thought blood bought loyalty. Didn't see his son slipping out the back."

Pause.

"Truth is, he thought Kris would follow him into that alley. He didn't."

Another pause.

"And the last thing Valon saw was that. Not a gun. Not the guy who shot him. Just the space where Kris should've been."

Twelve seconds.

That's all it took.

By sunrise, it had crossed platforms.

Forums. Telegram groups. Podcasts. Insta reels with stock dramatic music.

People paired it with old footage of Kris talking about "carrying the legacy."

They captioned it with:

"You didn't carry it. You dropped it."

"Bloodlines don't lie. But they leak."

•

Kris woke to 100 missed messages.

Two calls from Ermi.

None from Ade.

He stared at his screen like it had insulted him in his sleep.

Opened the clip.

Listened to it three times.

Didn't blink.

Didn't cry.

Just said, to no one:

"F—ing Maya."

•

But Maya hadn't named herself.

She hadn't promoted it.

She hadn't even spoken.

She just hit upload… and waited.

•

Ade was in his flat when the clip hit.

Ermi sent it in silence. No subject line.

Ade played it once.

Then again.

Then sat still long enough for the tea on the counter to go cold.

He didn't call Kris.

Didn't call Maya.

Didn't speak.

But inside, the silence shifted.

And it wasn't peace.

It was preparation.

Somewhere in Bethnal Green, a wall that used to advertise sneakers now read:

"VALON'S BLOOD RUNS THIN"

Spray paint. All caps. Fresh.

Chapter 7 - No Allegiance

The old school had no lights, no heat, and no locks that worked properly. But it had a roof. And four brick walls. And no press.

That was enough for Kris.

He stepped through a side door forced open with a crowbar earlier in the week, his hoodie soaked from the drizzle. The floors were cold and warped. Every door creaked like it remembered children. Somewhere deep in the halls, a fire alarm blinked uselessly, still powered by a dying backup battery.

This had been his Year 4 building. Miss Calloway's class. The smell of pencils and sweat and kids pretending not to cry. It was weird, being back. The kind of weird that didn't make you nostalgic — just tired.

He dumped his bag beside an overturned desk and kicked the legs out from under a rusty chair. Sat. Checked his phone.

No messages.

Again.

The screen was cracked from the poker night. He tapped through his contacts. Most names blurred together now — tags from backchannels, burner numbers, aliases from forums. He hit CALL on four. Got silence from all.

Then he tried someone real.

Ade.

It rang. Just once.

Then stopped.

Kris exhaled through his nose, opened the voice memo app, and started speaking.

"I know you saw it. The clip. Ermi's voice. The way they cut it. The way they made it sound. I never—"

"I didn't walk away that night. I hesitated. Yeah. But I didn't f—ing run."

Pause.

"You know how many nights I dream about that alley? How many times I've—"

Long silence.

"Forget it."

He deleted the message before saving it.

The quiet snapped shut around him again.

⸱

Outside, the rain picked up.

He stood under the broken window near the headteacher's office, watching the street blur into wet shapes. Once, people would've swarmed him for a selfie here. Now? They walked past like he was already a headline they'd scrolled past.

His name had stopped trending two days ago.

Replaced by a meme of his face mid-sentence, eyes half-shut, with the caption:

"This you?"

Kris sat back down and lit the last cigarette he had. The flame caught his fingers before the end lit properly. He didn't flinch.

⸱

He stared at the ceiling and whispered to no one:

"Still here."

But no one answered.

The room used to be a snooker hall — now converted into something half-way between a shrine and a storeroom. Low light. Cigarette haze. Red cloth draped over the pool tables. Bottles of Turkish raki lined up like offerings. In one corner, a small table with a single black-and-white photo: Valon Marku, framed in glass, eyes sharp even in grayscale.

No speeches. No press.

Just nods.

Just presence.

Ermi stood near the entrance in his long coat, arms crossed over a pigeon-feather scarf. The old crew were there — men who'd run money, moved guns, dug shallow holes in the wrong kind of rain. None of them greeted each other loudly. No one laughed.

Ade entered alone.

No coat. No umbrella. Just the quiet heaviness he always carried when the past was watching.

Someone handed him a glass.

He didn't drink from it.

He walked to the photo. Looked down. Said nothing.

Then turned — and saw her.

Maya.

Standing near the back wall, hands in pockets, eyes scanning the room like she didn't want to land on anyone too long. She wore black. Not mourning black. Journalist black. Neutral. Fitting in without implying she belonged.

Their eyes met.

He walked over slowly.

"You weren't invited," he said.

"I know."

"Then why come?"

"Because I recorded him," she said. "And because I might've buried him again."

Ade looked away.

Maya added, "I didn't tag your name. Or Kris's."

"You didn't need to."

They stood in silence, the murmurs of old men weaving around them.

Maya pulled something from her bag. Not a mic. Not a phone. A small square — a photo. A scan of a handwritten note. Ade glanced down.

It was a clipped quote from Valon, scribbled in jagged, impatient ink:

"If the world's gonna eat your name, make sure it chokes."

She held it up.

"I found it in the archive," she said. "You ever hear him say that?"

Ade nodded once.

Then handed it back.

Maya hesitated, then asked:

"You still think you can pull him out?"

Ade's face didn't change.

"I think Kris already chose the hole."

"And you?"

He looked her dead in the eye.

"Don't follow me after this."

Maya opened her mouth to say something — but Ade was already gone, disappearing into the crowd of men who still walked like soldiers and drank like ghosts.

Later that night, Kris scrolled through a livestream someone tagged him in.

A shaky phone video of the memorial.

He paused on one frame.

Ade.

Standing by the photo.

Expression unreadable.

Kris watched that ten-second clip seventeen times.

Then turned his phone off.

The door wasn't smashed — it was unlocked.

Maya knew that because she always triple-locked it. She knew the exact sound of each bolt sliding home. She knew the feel of it in her hand — and the slight twist required to keep the bottom latch from sticking.

She also knew the cold weight that dropped into her chest the moment she walked in and felt something off.

The air was… too still.

Her mic was on the floor, cord curled like a question mark.

The room looked undisturbed — almost surgical. No drawers yanked open. No mess. But her laptop was unplugged. Her backup drives were missing from their Velcro-lined case. Her whiteboard had been wiped clean.

Except for one thing.

A red circle, drawn with a dry-erase marker, thick and aggressive.

Around one word.

ERMI.

Maya stood still for a moment, trying to control her breathing.

Then she moved through the room like it belonged to someone else. Checked her shelves. Her files. The lockbox with the old mini-recorders — untouched.

Whoever had come through here knew exactly what they were looking for.

And they'd found some of it.

But not all of it.

Her phone buzzed just before 3:00 p.m.

Unknown Number.

No name. Just a message.

"You're not the only one who wants the truth."

And then, a second:

"He talks to ghosts. I used to run with them."

Attached: a voice file.

Ten seconds of distorted audio. Background noise. Water. Breathing.

And one clear sentence:

"Lenny didn't want Valon dead. He wanted Kris to think someone else did."

No timestamp. No ID.

Maya played it three times. Her hands didn't stop shaking.

She typed back:

"Who are you?"

No reply.

Instead, her laptop pinged — an auto-synced file from a dead Google Drive account.

A document appeared. Titled:

"PROJECT BLEACH."

She didn't open it.

Not yet.

She sat down in her chair and stared at the circle around ERMI until the ink began to smear in her mind.

⸻

Outside the building, someone in a black puffer jacket lit a cigarette and crossed her name off a damp, folded list.

No rush.

The garage was half-collapsed, its metal roof bowing in like a bruised lung.

It used to belong to one of their uncles — or maybe a cousin — but now it was just another forgotten square in a city full of them. No working lights. No neighbours to hear anything. Perfect for things you didn't want explained later.

Ade stood in the middle, still as a statue, arms folded.

The boy sat on an oil drum, zip ties around his wrists, hoodie pushed back to show a fresh bruise along his jaw. Late teens. Twitchy. Clothes too clean to be broke, but too loose to be expensive. He hadn't spoken since he'd been pulled into the van two hours earlier.

Ade crouched in front of him.

No shouting. No threat in his voice.

"You know who I am?"

The boy nodded.

"You know why you're here?"

Another nod.

Ade waited. Then, softly:

"Say it."

The boy swallowed. His voice cracked.

"I passed Kris's location."

"To who?"

"I don't know. I swear. Burner account. Said they were fans. Wanted to know where he was hiding."

Ade tilted his head slightly.

"Fans don't pay in crypto."

The boy flinched.

Ade stood, walked a slow circle around him, voice steady:

"You think this is about snitching? It's not. You think this is about loyalty? Still wrong. This is about timing."

The boy blinked.

"Timing?"

Ade stopped behind him.

"If Kris goes down now, he looks like a tragedy. If he goes down later — when I'm ready — he looks like a plan."

He leaned down. Quiet.

"And I don't like improvisation."

The boy's breath came faster.

"You gonna kill me?"

Ade didn't answer.

Instead, he stepped into the light near the shutter. Pulled something from his pocket — the boy's phone. Scrolled. Showed him the screen.

"Recognize the contact?"

The boy hesitated. Then: "Yeah."

Ade tapped the screen, deleted the entire chain of messages.

Then tossed the phone into a puddle across the floor.

"Here's what's going to happen," he said. "You're going to walk out of here. You're going to forget who you spoke to. And if someone asks? You got jumped. No faces. No story. Just silence."

The boy looked confused.

"I'm not dead?"

Ade's expression didn't shift.

"No. You're useful."

He cut the zip ties, slow and deliberate.

The boy stood, wrists red and slick with nervous sweat.

He didn't run.

He just left.

Ade waited a full minute after the door shut before moving again.

Then, alone, he said aloud:

"Two more holes to dig."

And picked up the shovel in the corner.

The rooftop was slick with rain and pigeon shit, and smelled faintly of burning insulation.

Kris stood near the edge, arms folded against the wind, watching the city flicker beneath a low, gunmetal sky. He hadn't shaved. His trainers were dirty. The hoodie was the same one from the fight night. He hadn't changed it in three days.

A metal door creaked behind him.

Boots stepped into view.

Rin.

Old fixer. Used to run transit IDs and fake border docs for Valon back when they were still shipping counterfeit cigarettes through embassy trucks. Still wore leather gloves. Still didn't smile.

She handed him a cigarette. No lighter. Just the cigarette.

"Got you a clean name," she said. "No digital footprint. NHS number, provisional license, burner line. One-way ticket out tomorrow morning. Belgium, then Albania, if you don't f— it up."

Kris didn't take the cig. Just stared at the river.

"How much?"

"Already paid."

"By who?"

Rin stared. "You know who."

He laughed — not loud, not full. Just a bitter exhale.

"Ade."

She didn't answer.

He finally took the cigarette. Lit it off a Zippo etched with a crest he didn't recognize.

"You think I'll go?" he asked.

"I don't think anything," Rin said. "I just build exits."

Kris inhaled. Let it out slow.

"You ever leave?"

"Three times."

"And?"

She shrugged. "Left the wrong bits behind."

He didn't say anything for a while.

Then:

"You ever wish you'd stayed?"

She looked at him like he'd asked the wrong question.

"No," she said. "I wish I'd left sooner."

A long pause.

Kris flicked ash over the edge of the roof.

"I thought if I kept moving, it'd mean something."

"It did," Rin said. "To everyone else. Just not to you."

He nodded once. Then turned, walking toward the door.

"Thanks for the papers."

"Don't thank me."

She stayed behind as he disappeared into the stairwell.

⸱

Kris stepped into the alley below the warehouse, hands in his pockets, cigarette still burning.

He didn't see the figure at first — they were leaning against the brick wall, hood up, shoes planted wide, a bulge beneath the jacket that didn't look like a phone.

Kris slowed.

They didn't move.

Then they looked up.

Not a stranger.

Not a cop.

Someone who used to owe Valon money — and had a reason to hate both Marku brothers now.

"You got a minute?" the figure asked.

Kris stopped.

Didn't answer.

Didn't smile.

Just watched the glint of metal in the figure's hand reflect a passing headlight.

And said:

"Not really."

Chapter 8 - Exit Wounds

The figure stepped forward, slow and deliberate, like someone who'd already rehearsed this walk.

Kris stayed where he was — three steps from the fire exit, five from the street, maybe seven from the end of something that had once felt immortal. His hands were in his pockets. One held a lighter. The other clenched around nothing.

The figure stopped just out of swing range.

Hood still up.

Blade now visible.

Short. Serrated. Not new.

"You don't remember me," the man said.

Kris's eyes scanned — gait, build, accent.

"I do," he said, evenly. "Your brother owed my dad ten grand in '08. Paid it in watches."

The blade twitched up slightly.

"You still talk like you own the city."

"I don't," Kris said. "But it still remembers my footprints."

The man stepped closer. Close enough for Kris to smell the cigarettes in his breath. Menthol. Cheap.

"You laughed on camera while Lenny's blood bled out. You gonna laugh now?"

"No," Kris said. "Not today."

A silence hung. Heavy as concrete.

The man's eyes narrowed. "You're not even gonna beg?"

Kris shook his head. "No. I'm gonna remind you of two things."

The man raised the knife, just slightly.

"First," Kris said, "your cousin Rafi still owes me four favours. Real ones. No cash, no threats — favours. You kill me, he dies choking on his own tongue next week."

The man didn't blink. Kris leaned in, just enough.

"And second — if you do this now, you'll be the punchline to someone else's story. You won't be remembered as the man who killed a king. You'll be the desperate footnote that got deleted in the edit."

The blade hung between them, uncertain now.

One long second.

Two.

Then—

The man stepped back.

Still holding the knife.

But not swinging.

"You're lucky," he muttered.

"No," Kris said. "I'm aware."

The man turned and disappeared into the alley's shadow, footsteps fading fast.

Kris waited. Didn't move.

Then, slowly, he exhaled.

And only then did he notice the pain in his thigh — a shallow graze, warm blood slicking his jeans.

He hadn't even felt it.

He limped out onto the street, past puddles and bins and broken neon. No swagger. Just breath.

His phone buzzed.

UNKNOWN NUMBER

One message:

"Next one won't hesitate."

⬚

Kris stared at the screen, then opened the front-facing camera.

His face was pale. Mouth tight.

And behind the fear…

Something else.

That old, electric hunger.

The one that came right before he did something reckless.

He snapped a photo.

Captioned it.

Posted it.

"Still breathing. Still building."

Then tossed the phone into a bin.

And walked into the night like it owed him change.

The basement smelled like sweat, bleach, and old anger.

Somewhere overhead, the city breathed normally — buses stopping, phones ringing, music leaking from headphones. But down here, under the halal butcher on Sclater Street, it was just the dim hum of strip lights and the muffled slap of fists into leather.

Ade stepped through the security door flanked by two large men in tracksuits, both of them too still to be anything but bored and dangerous. He was told nothing. No escort. No warning.

Just walked through a narrow corridor of rusted pipes and condensation, and then:

The ring.

Taped, sagging ropes. Canvas floor dark with stains that didn't all come from sparring. Four chairs against the wall. One folding table. No audience.

Just Lenny Uzun, seated on a stool at the far side of the ring, sipping from a paper cup. Dressed sharp. Stone grey suit. No tie.

"You brought gloves?" he said casually.

Ade stopped two metres away.

"I thought this was a conversation."

"It is," Lenny said. "Just not a verbal one."

He nodded toward the far corner.

A man stood up — tall, lean, a boxer's build under a sleeveless hoodie. Ade didn't recognize him. But the way he rolled his wrists told the story: trained. Controlled. Eager.

"Get in," Lenny said.

Ade didn't move.

"I'm not your fighter."

"No," Lenny said. "You're a man with too much history and not enough present. Let's change that."

The man in the ring stretched his neck side to side. Bounced lightly. Waiting.

Ade looked around. There were no cameras.

"Am I proving something to you," he asked, "or to him?"

"To yourself," Lenny said. "To me, you've always been a maybe."

A long beat passed.

Then Ade stepped up onto the apron.

Dropped his coat.

No gloves.

Just knuckles and intent.

⸱

The bell wasn't real — someone just smacked a metal pipe with a wrench.

The first punch came fast — a jab straight to the ribs. Ade moved with it. Absorbed the second. Let the third hit air.

Then he returned one.

Quick. Low. Clean.

Blood from the nose.

The fighter smiled.

Ade didn't.

⸱

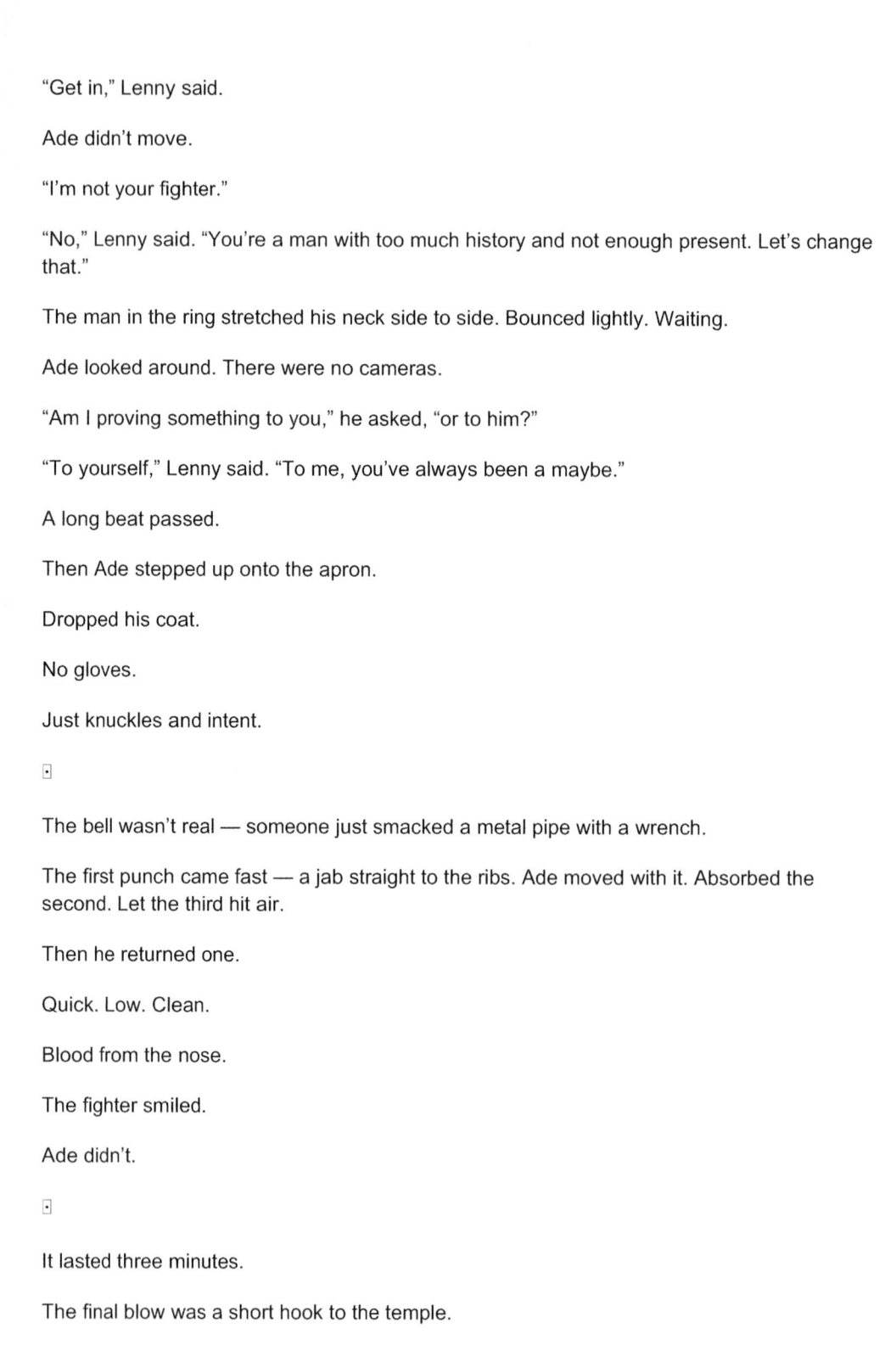

It lasted three minutes.

The final blow was a short hook to the temple.

Not enough to kill.

But enough to make the man forget his postcode.

He dropped hard.

Lenny didn't clap.

Just sipped from his cup.

Ade stepped back, breathing steady, sweat darkening his collar.

No words exchanged.

Just the sound of the pipe clanging again. The round was over.

The message wasn't.

Lenny stood.

Walked to the ropes.

Leaned on them.

"Only reason you're not like your brother," he said, "is you know when to bleed."

Ade wiped his mouth. "You finished testing me?"

"No," Lenny said. "Next test comes when you choose. Him or me."

Then he left the basement without looking back.

⁂

Ade stayed in the ring a moment longer.

Looked down at his fists.

Still his.

For now.

The studio was dark but alive — like a severed limb still twitching.

Maya sat in the center, ringed by monitors, hard drives, notes, thumb drives labeled in Sharpie. A half-eaten takeaway box perched on top of a speaker. One tea gone cold. The other untouched.

On screen:

Timeline: DEATH OF VALON MARKU

▷ FILE 01 – Ermi Interview (Uncut)

▷ FILE 03 – Police Audio Leak

▷ FILE 05 – Maya's Rooftop Conversation w/ Ade

▷ FILE 06 – Kris: "He Died A Legend" (Promo Clip)

▷ FILE 07 – CCTV Extract: Alley Entry, 2009

▷ FILE 09 – Forensics Map Overlay

▷ FILE 10 – Unreleased Funeral Audio

She didn't speak as she clicked through them.

She didn't breathe deeply until she got to FILE 05.

Ade's voice. Calm. Low. Older than it had any right to sound.

ADE (recorded):

"He asked Kris to follow. He waited in that alley like it was a test. But Kris never showed. That's not murder. That's abandonment."

She rewound. Played it again.

There it was — intention.

Not just silence. Not just myth.

Guilt.

She opened her editing software. Dragged the waveform across the screen like a blade. Cut. Spliced. Matched it to old footage — Kris at the funeral, standing in front of the casket, delivering a prewritten speech about family, loyalty, legend.

Overlayed it with the police leak.

Overlayed that with Ermi's raw interview:

"Valon was trying to hand over the crown. But Kris only wanted the robe."

She added a title card:

"TRUTH ISN'T LOYAL."

Then encrypted the file.

Password-protected it.

Backed it up in three locations.

One on a server in Iceland.

One on a flash drive in her boot.

One in the hands of someone she hadn't spoken to in two years.

She sat back.

Looked at the rendered file.

Then whispered:

"Now someone decides who burns."

Just as she moved to close her laptop—

A knock.

Soft.

Two knocks. Then three.

Rhythmic. Intentional.

She didn't move.

The screen flickered.

Another knock. Louder.

She reached under the desk.

Felt the can of pepper spray taped to the bottom panel.

Another knock.

Then a voice. Male. Muffled through the door.

"It's not a threat."

Pause.

"It's a favour."

Her hand froze.

The waveform still pulsed on the screen behind her.

And outside, the truth had started walking toward her door.

The stairwell stank of piss and lost names.

Fifth floor. No lights. The walls were tag-patched and peeling — old gang signs scribbled over with newer warnings. Some of the doors had been welded shut. Others had been kicked in and left that way.

Ade stepped over a broken pram frame and walked down the hall until he found the open unit. Flat 52C. The door was ajar, wedged open with a brick.

He stepped inside.

No furniture. No heat.

Just Ermi, sitting on an upside-down milk crate, wearing a black bomber and a face like unfinished grief.

He didn't rise.

Didn't offer a seat.

"Ade," he said. "Come in."

Ade closed the door behind him.

Ermi nodded to the floor beside him — a cracked slab of tile. Resting on it: a folded cloth. Black. Soft. Heavy with implication.

"Sit," Ermi said. "Or stand. Just don't pretend we've got time."

Ade didn't sit.

He looked at the cloth.

"You're too old for theatre," he said.

"I'm old enough to know how stories end," Ermi replied.

A gust of wind howled through the broken window.

"You know what I hate about your generation?" Ermi said. "You think silence is strategy. That if you don't speak, no one can trace the blood back to you."

He leaned forward, eyes sharp.

"But blood leaks. Even through sealed lips."

Ade said nothing.

Ermi pulled something from his jacket — an old photo. Faded. Torn along one edge.

It showed the Marku brothers as teenagers, standing on a roof with Valon. Kris was already posing like he was someone. Ade had his head down.

"He made you both in his image," Ermi said. "One for war, one for witness. You were meant to survive him. Kris? He was just supposed to echo."

Ade stared at the photo.

"You think I can stop him?"

Ermi snorted.

"No. I think you already decided not to. I think you're just waiting for the world to punish him so you don't have to feel like a traitor."

He picked up the black cloth. Unfolded it. Inside: a short, compact pistol. Old. Worn. The kind used to end arguments, not start them.

"Lenny won't ask again," Ermi said. "If you don't make a move, he will. And you know what his kind of moves look like."

He held out the gun.

"Make it quick. Make it private. Make it clean."

Ade didn't move.

But his hands curled into fists at his sides.

Ermi set the gun on the crate between them.

"If you don't want the crown," he said, "fine. But don't pretend you weren't born in the palace."

⸰

They stood there. Silence deep and raw.

Then Ade stepped forward.

Picked up the gun.

No expression.

Just weight.

Ermi watched him leave the flat without another word.

The sound of his boots echoed down the ruined hall, like punctuation.

The restaurant was calm, almost reverent.

Low lights. Floral tilework. Quiet families murmuring over grilled lamb and aubergine. A radio played an old Turkish ballad too softly to follow. Waiters moved like shadows, smooth and practiced.

The boy had come alone. Skinny. Nervous. Barely old enough to drink. Hoodie tucked into itself. Head down. He sat at a table near the kitchen, ordered nothing but tea, and disappeared into the bathroom ten minutes later.

He didn't come out.

Not after five minutes.

Not after ten.

At twenty, the waiter knocked once. Got no answer. Opened the door.

And screamed.

⸺

The body was slumped against the back wall.

No signs of a struggle.

Just one deep wound under the ribcage — clean, almost surgical. The blood had pooled neatly beneath him, soaking into the grout like spilled wine. His face was calm. Like he'd known. Like he'd made peace.

Pinned to his chest with a cocktail skewer:

"THIS WAS MERCY."

⸺

No cameras in the bathroom.

None working in the hallway.

By the time the police arrived, no one remembered seeing him enter. No one remembered seeing anyone else follow. The place had been packed. Quiet. Innocent.

They bagged the body. Took statements.

And said very little.

⸺

Word hit the street within the hour.

Not just who it was — a boy who'd been whispering Kris's whereabouts to someone bigger, louder, more dangerous — but how it was done.

The how spread faster than the why.

Ade got the message from Ermi.

A photo of the scene. Blurred. Bleached under flash.

His only response:

"Not me."

Kris heard about it two hours later — through an anonymous burner message with just one image attached.

The note.

No explanation.

He stared at it for a long time.

Then whispered:

"Ade…"

Neither called the other.

Neither denied it.

Both started sleeping with the lights on.

Chapter 9 - Blood Echo

The club hadn't pulsed in years.

Kris pushed open the side entrance with his shoulder, flashlight clutched between his teeth, stepping into the hollow ribs of what used to be PULSE — Valon's first money-laundering operation before the gyms, before the fight circuits, before the war.

It was all still there, somehow.

The twisted mirror wall. The DJ booth scrawled with marker tags and phone numbers. A pair of ruined speakers sagging from the ceiling like vultures that lost interest. Even the sticky floor, lacquered with a decade of spilled vodka, cheap perfume, and adrenaline.

Kris exhaled and stepped behind the bar. The dust lit up like fog in his flashlight beam.

This was the first place Valon ever took him after a job. He'd sat Kris on a stool, poured him orange juice in a whisky glass, and said:

"People don't fear what you say. They fear what you're willing to be quiet about."

Back then, it had sounded like scripture.

Now it just sounded like a curse.

He set his bag down, checked the makeshift lock on the side door — a snapped broom handle wedged against the hinge. Not perfect. But it'd slow someone down.

He pulled out a granola bar, unwrapped it slowly, sat on a milk crate near the broken light rig.

Halfway through chewing, he heard it.

A footstep.

Too light to be Ermi. Too quick to be police.

He turned the flashlight.

A kid.

Fourteen? Maybe fifteen. Skinny. Trainers too clean. Hoodie too big. Something clutched in his pocket.

Kris stood.

The kid froze, caught in the beam.

"You're him," he said. "Aren't you?"

Kris didn't answer.

"I saw you fight that night," the boy said. "You were live. I clipped it. I reposted it. Got like nine hundred likes."

Still, Kris said nothing.

The kid edged closer. "They say you killed that boy with one hit. That true?"

Kris stepped out from behind the bar. Quiet. Careful.

"You here alone?" he asked.

The kid smiled. "What, you worried I'm the police?"

"No," Kris said. "I'm worried you're not."

The boy took another step. He wasn't scared. He was buzzing. High on proximity. He pulled something from his hoodie — not a knife, not a gun.

His phone.

"Can I—" he started.

Kris moved fast.

Snatched the phone before the boy could raise it. Slammed it face-down on the bar and cracked the back open with his palm.

"Oi!" the kid yelped. "What the f—?"

Kris held up the device, peeled out the SIM card, and crushed it under his boot.

"You know what happens to kids who find me?" he said. "They stop being kids."

The boy backed off now. His eyes were wide. "I wasn't— I just wanted to— I didn't know—"

Kris stepped forward.

"This isn't a story," he hissed. "It's a burial. Get out. Now."

The boy turned and bolted through the side door, his footsteps slapping echoes into the hollow dark.

Kris stood there alone.

The broken phone still ticking faintly in his hand like a dying heart.

·

Later that night, he pulled an old crate to the middle of the floor, sat cross-legged like a monk, and stared up at the disco ball — still dangling, still turning in the draft like it remembered being something brighter.

He whispered to it:

"You ever want to be forgotten?"

The silence didn't answer.

But it stayed.

The evidence lockup smelled like cardboard and disinfectant — a place where secrets went to grow dust.

Maya signed the waiver with a dry pen, using a name she hadn't used in three years. The constable on duty didn't look at her twice. Just buzzed her in, handed her a clipboard, and pointed to Vault C.

No one escorted her.

Nobody asked what she was looking for.

That was the trick — hide the truth in plain, forgotten boxes.

Row after row of steel shelves stretched into the shadows, each lined with dull plastic crates marked in felt-tip: HGV STING, DOCK RAID, REDACTED, STABBING – NO CPS.

She stopped when she found the box marked:

MARKU / DECEASED / 2009

(Archive Reference: 998.42.A-V)

It was lighter than expected. Inside:

- One bloody shirt
- One half-burned pack of Sobranie Black Russians
- One mini DV tape in a cracked plastic case, labeled in biro:

NIGHT / 01-14 / ALLEY-CCTV

Maya slipped the tape into her coat pocket like it was a live round.

Back in her flat — all locks double-checked, blinds drawn, spray can by the door — she dragged her old camcorder out of a storage box. Plugged in the adapter. The screen flickered like a dying eye.

She loaded the tape.

Pressed play.

The footage was rough. No audio. Just grainy black and white, timestamped in the corner.

01:07am.

An alleyway she'd only ever seen in crime reports. Narrow. Boxy. Dim.

Valon appeared first. Alone. Coat flapping. He looked… calm.

Then: someone else.

Not Kris.

Not Ade.

A third man. Built like a fighter. Face shadowed. Walked like he owned oxygen.

He and Valon talked. No gestures. No yelling. Just proximity. A lean-in.

Then —

A flash of movement.

Valon stumbles.

The man steps back, tosses something — maybe a gun — behind a bin.

Walks away. Fast. Not running.

Then…

Kris appears.

Thirty seconds later.

He reaches Valon's body.

Kneels.

Hands shaking.

And sits there. Still. For a long time.

Maya paused the footage. Rewound.

The third man.

Frame by frame.

When he turned just enough for a partial profile—

Her breath stopped.

She knew that face.

Not from crime reports.

From interviews.

From Valon's old crew.

From Kris's own fight circuit promos.

"Holy shit," she whispered.

She pressed her forehead to the cool edge of the desk.

There was someone else at that alley.

Someone everyone had been protecting.

And she had the tape.

⸱

She encrypted it.

Doubled the backups.

Then sat in the dark, eyes wide, laptop fan humming like a nervous breath.

Outside, a car parked across the street.

Engine idling.

No one got out.

The car was already idling when Maya stepped onto the curb.

She didn't see Ade until he opened the passenger door from inside, just a crack.

"Maya," he said. Calm. Controlled. Like this wasn't an ambush, but a meeting they'd both agreed to in another life.

She froze, keys tight in her fist.

He nodded to the seat.

"I'm not armed."

"Great," she said. "That makes one of us."

But she got in.

Door shut. Lock clicked.

They sat in silence for a moment, the rain ticking softly against the windscreen.

Maya didn't look at him.

"You know what I found," she said flatly.

"Yes."

"You know what's on that tape."

"Yes."

She turned now, staring. "Then why aren't you trying to take it from me?"

Ade stared forward, hands on the wheel like they were keeping him here.

"Because if I take it, you'll scream. If I ask for it, you might listen."

Maya waited.

"What do you want to trade?" she asked.

Ade finally turned.

His face was unreadable. But something in it looked fractured.

"I'll tell you what happened when Kris was fifteen."

Maya blinked. "That's not the deal I—"

"It is now."

A beat.

Then she leaned back, arms folded.

"Talk."

⸰

Ade didn't rush.

"Kris was supposed to start running drop-offs that year. Nothing big. Phones, envelopes, sometimes just showing up to be seen."

He exhaled through his nose.

"Valon had him tagged as the next version of himself. Loud. Ruthless. Charming. People liked Kris — and Valon hated needing to rely on anyone people liked."

Maya tilted her head slightly. "You jealous?"

"No," Ade said. "I was relieved."

He looked out the window.

"But then came the drop. Some footage — not even valuable. Just old CCTV of a fight that Lenny lost. Kris was meant to deliver it to a buyer. Simple handoff."

Maya narrowed her eyes. "And?"

"Kris never showed."

"Why?"

"Because he sold it first. To someone else. Took cash up front, then fed the buyer a blank tape."

Maya blinked. "Wait — Kris conned someone? At fifteen?"

Ade nodded.

"It was messy. Loud. Got back to Valon in a day."

"What happened?"

Ade's voice lowered.

"He beat Kris in front of the entire crew. Stripped him of his cut. Told him: 'If you're gonna lie, lie better.'"

Maya looked stunned.

Ade didn't stop.

"From then on, Valon saw him as a gamble. Not a son. Not a successor. Just a wild card. So when Kris didn't show that night in the alley—"

"He expected it," Maya finished. "He'd already stopped believing."

Ade nodded once.

Then reached into his coat. Slowly.

He didn't pull a weapon.

Just a USB stick.

"This is everything I have left," he said. "My own version. Not edited. Not spun. No legacy in it. Just rot."

He held it out.

Maya didn't take it right away.

"And the tape?" Ade asked.

"I still have it."

He nodded.

"Don't share it yet."

She stared at him.

"You protecting him, or yourself?"

"Doesn't matter now," he said.

And turned the engine off.

Maya stepped out into the rain, USB still clutched in her hand.

She didn't look back.

Neither did he.

The gym smelled like promise — and bleach.

Sweat and floor cleaner. Blood, maybe, somewhere beneath the mats.

Valon Marku Memorial Youth Invitational was printed in faded black vinyl over the entrance arch. The ring was scuffed. The gloves were borrowed. The kids were real.

Kris kept his hood up as he slid in through the side door. No cameras. No spotlight. Just seats half-filled with cousins, old trainers, shopkeepers who used to slide him free Lucozade when he was fourteen and punching shadows.

He kept to the edge of the bleachers, back to the wall.

He wasn't sure why he'd come.

Somewhere in him, the past still buzzed with unfinished songs.

The first match ended — a scrappy win for a tall kid with fast hands and no defense. The bell rang. Applause. Water bottles. Coaches shouting praise like gospel.

Kris started to leave.

Then someone turned.

A kid. Thirteen, maybe. Thin as a broom handle. Hair cut sharp. Jacket too big.

The kid froze.

Whispered something to the boy next to him.

Both turned.

And then: the whisper ripple.

Kris Marku.

That's him.

He's here.

A few of the older boys didn't approach.

But one did.

He stepped forward like it was an altar.

"Can I—" he held up a phone. "Just one?"

Kris didn't smile. But he nodded.

The flash popped.

The kid stared at him like he was the moon.

"You gonna start a gym again?" he asked. "We heard you might. My cousin said you might be looking for sparring heads."

Kris didn't answer.

The kid looked behind him, then leaned closer.

"They say Lenny's got new boys in Tower Hamlets. They're watching your name. But if you came back…"

He didn't finish the sentence.

Kris put a hand on his shoulder.

Squeezed once.

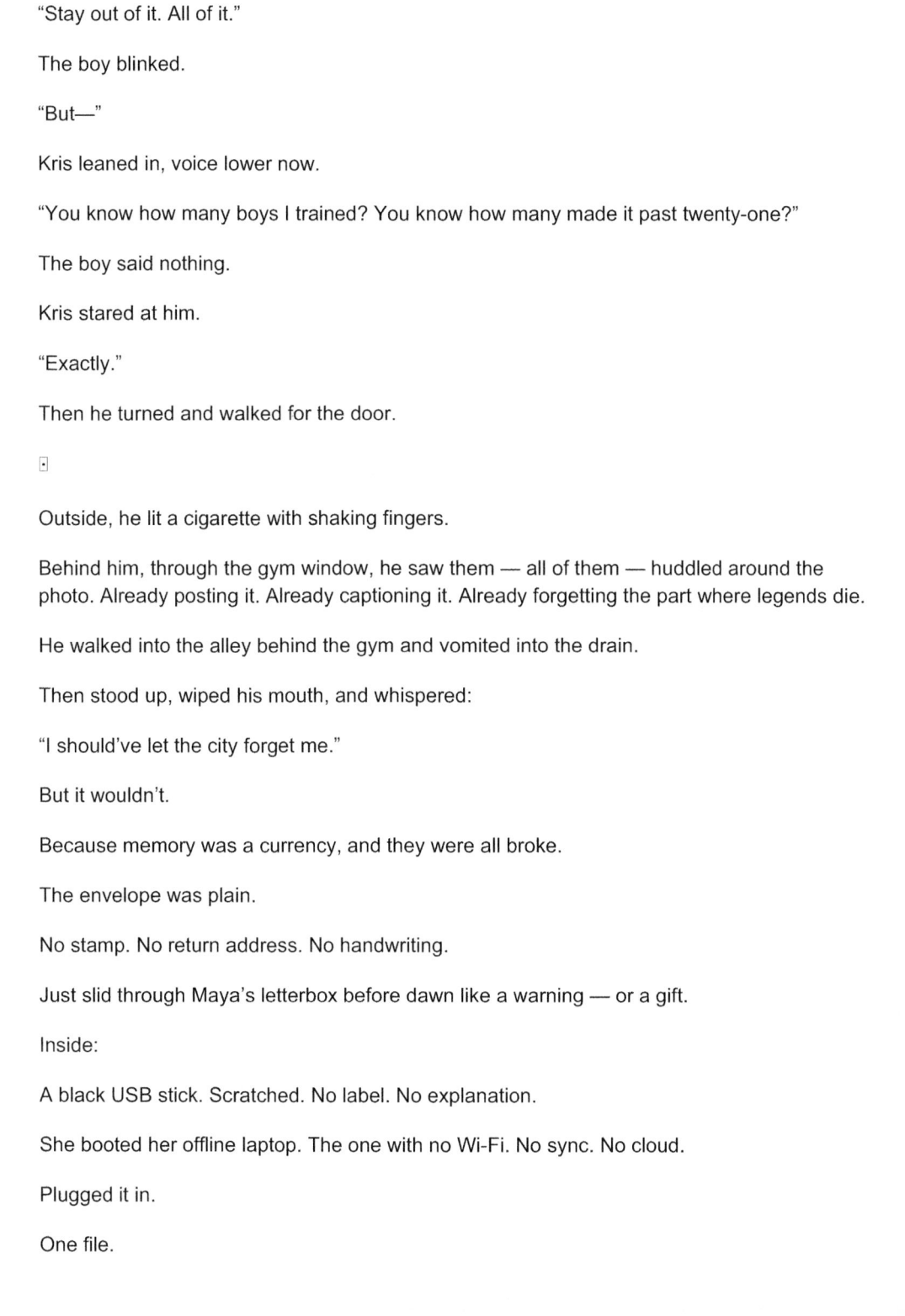

Then said, softly:

"Stay out of it. All of it."

The boy blinked.

"But—"

Kris leaned in, voice lower now.

"You know how many boys I trained? You know how many made it past twenty-one?"

The boy said nothing.

Kris stared at him.

"Exactly."

Then he turned and walked for the door.

⸱

Outside, he lit a cigarette with shaking fingers.

Behind him, through the gym window, he saw them — all of them — huddled around the photo. Already posting it. Already captioning it. Already forgetting the part where legends die.

He walked into the alley behind the gym and vomited into the drain.

Then stood up, wiped his mouth, and whispered:

"I should've let the city forget me."

But it wouldn't.

Because memory was a currency, and they were all broke.

The envelope was plain.

No stamp. No return address. No handwriting.

Just slid through Maya's letterbox before dawn like a warning — or a gift.

Inside:

A black USB stick. Scratched. No label. No explanation.

She booted her offline laptop. The one with no Wi-Fi. No sync. No cloud.

Plugged it in.

One file.

"LAST_VOICENOTE.wav"

She clicked play.

The audio crackled with background noise — wind, maybe, or the hum of a car heater.

Then:

Valon Marku's voice.

Older than most recordings. Slower. Like he was trying to say something without saying everything.

"If this reaches anyone… I guess I didn't finish what I started."

Pause.

"I raised two boys. One who watched too much. One who spoke too fast. I thought maybe they'd fix each other, the way broken mirrors make one image. But mirrors lie."

More static. A cough.

"I did wrong by them. Thought I could make the fire burn clean if I handed it down dressed as legacy. But I made a bomb, not a bloodline."

Maya's hands tightened on the edges of the laptop.

"If you're hearing this, you want truth. You want blood. You want to pin something to someone. Maybe both."

Another pause.

"Kris… wanted the crown before he understood the weight. Ade… carried the weight but never reached for it. And then there's the one neither of them saw coming."

Valon's voice drops.

Almost a whisper.

"If anyone survives me, it'll be Levan. Because Levan never wanted the light. Just the silence it came with."

Click.

The file ended.

No time stamp. No metadata. No location tag.

Just a name.

Levan.

Maya sat frozen.

She'd interviewed every member of Valon's known crew.

Levan never came up.

He wasn't in the reports.

Not in the tapes.

Not in the death.

But Valon had left the truth in a whisper.

And now that whisper was ticking like a fuse.

She copied the file three times.

Encrypted it.

And started searching.

Outside her flat, parked across the street, the same engine idled quietly.

Still waiting.

Chapter 10 - The Third Brother

The gym was dead.

No lights. No bags. No sounds except the creak of old rope and the drip-drip of a leaking roof into a rusted mop bucket near the ring.

Kris slipped through the side door, shoulders hunched. The moment he stepped inside, it hit him — that smell: sweat and floor wax, blood gone stale, chalk ground into the mat. His father's scent. Still lingering.

This was Valon's first gym. Before the fights were ticketed. Before the names meant anything. Before the crew wore black gloves and gold rings. Here, men bled for nothing. For pride. For practice.

He stepped into the ring. The canvas gave slightly under his weight.

He sat.

Silence thick.

Then his boot nudged something.

A curl in the mat. Loose.

He pulled at it.

Underneath — dust, wrappers, old roach ends.

And a single envelope.

Yellowed.

Taped flat to the underside of the mat with black electrical tape, edges hard with age.

His name wasn't on it.

But the handwriting was unmistakable:

Valon's.

He peeled it off.

Opened it.

Inside: one photograph.

Three boys.

Teenagers, maybe sixteen. Standing in front of this very gym, arms crossed, eyes hard. One of them — unmistakably Kris, wearing a tracksuit three sizes too big. The second — Ade, smaller, looking off-camera.

The third — tall. Quiet eyes. Crooked teeth. Familiar in a way that made Kris's throat tighten.

Same brow.

Same cheekbones.

Different mouth.

Different aura.

Like he was built of something slower. Colder.

On the back of the photo, scrawled in faded biro:

"One to watch.

One to lead.

One to wait."

No names.

No date.

Kris stared at the third boy.

The not him. The not Ade.

He whispered aloud:

"Who the fuck are you?"

And in the hollow space of the gym, the echo answered back with nothing.

⸻

He left the ring. Didn't look back.

But he pocketed the photo.

And for the first time in months, he didn't feel angry.

He felt replaced.

The flat in Canning Town was wallpapered in old grime and fresh paranoia.

Maya sat opposite the woman — early sixties, scarf tied too tight around her neck, eyes that blinked too little. Jana Dervishi, name changed twice, last seen in a payroll sheet from Valon's club books in '09.

She hadn't agreed to the meeting easily. It took three burner calls, one envelope of cash, and a promise: no recording.

"You worked his books," Maya said, hands flat on the table.

"I sorted envelopes," Jana replied. "Don't dress it up."

"You were there the year before he died."

Jana shrugged. "So were a hundred other ghosts."

Maya slid the photo across the table — the one from under the mat.

Jana's eyes twitched.

"You recognize him," Maya said.

"Which one?"

Maya pointed. "The third."

Jana hesitated.

"Levan," she said finally. "Never spoke. Never ate with us. Never smiled. But he had a set of keys to Valon's second office. Only Valon and Ermi had those."

"What was he?"

"Furniture," Jana said. "That's how he made himself. Sat in the corner. Never interrupted. Always listening. Like a recorder."

"Blood?"

Jana shook her head. "Valon never said. But he kept him close."

"How close?"

Jana leaned forward.

"Close enough to trust him with messages Kris never got."

·

Maya's breath caught.

"What happened to him?"

Jana scratched at her scarf. Her voice dropped.

"He left after the funeral. Said nothing. Took nothing. I only heard his name once again. Two years later."

She pulled a folded paper from under the couch cushion. Slid it across.

It was an old invoice. Albanian address. Scribbled note across the top:

"L. Marku – bulk order, gloves + wraps"

Maya stared at the address.

"Is this where he went?"

"No," Jana said. "That's where they kept sending payments."

Maya blinked. "They?"

"Ermi," she said. "And sometimes Ade."

Maya sat back.

Everything rewired in her head.

"So he wasn't forgotten," she said. "He was protected."

Jana nodded once.

"By someone. Maybe by all of them."

Outside, Maya folded the invoice twice and slid it into her coat pocket.

The name Levan Marku now had geography.

Next would come motive.

Behind her, the curtains shifted — just slightly — though Jana never touched them.

The cemetery had the kind of silence that made you feel like a trespasser.

Rows of headstones bent in the soft earth, like they were leaning to listen. Most graves were adorned — flowers, plastic saints, little flags. But Valon Marku's was bare. Just a slab. Weather-faded. The inscription too short.

VALON MARKU

Father. Fighter. Flame.

1967–2009

Ade stood over it with his coat zipped halfway and one hand in his pocket. A drizzle spat against his shoulders, gentle but insistent.

He didn't visit often. Last time had been… what? Seven years ago? No reason, really. Just ran out of things to lie about.

Now, he knelt.

Fingers traced the grooves of the name.

Then, he spoke.

Soft. Not performative. Just tired.

"You never let anyone call you sentimental," he said. "But you kept three shoeboxes under your bed. One was photos. One was papers. The third was full of old gloves and a passport that didn't belong to you."

He paused.

"Levan's."

The name hung in the air like a bullet after firing — silent, but irreversibly real.

Ade kept going.

"You told me to never say it. Said the name was heavy. Said if it came out too early, it'd pull the house down."

He glanced around the cemetery. Empty.

"You trained him first, didn't you? Before Kris could throw a jab without closing his eyes. Before I learned to keep mine open."

He wiped rain from his brow.

"You knew Kris would try to wear your crown before he could carry it. And you knew I'd carry it without asking why."

Another pause.

"So you built Levan as the other option. The shadow. The backup flame."

A silence.

Then, with no emotion:

"I always hated you for that."

He stood.

Took a folded piece of paper from his coat pocket. The photo Kris had found — the three boys. He laid it gently on the grave, weighed down with a smooth stone.

"Someone's looking for him now," Ade murmured. "She's good. She'll find something. Maybe more than I want her to."

He looked down.

"I won't stop her."

Then, more quietly:

"But I won't protect you anymore either."

He walked away.

Didn't look back.

Behind the headstone, water pooled in a dip of earth.

The photo held in place.

The stone did not.

Ermi's burner was cheap. The kind you replace more often than you charge.

He kept it in the glovebox of a grey Toyota Corolla with no license plates, wrapped in a Crown Royal bag like it was carrying a relic.

That night, he powered it on to check a message from Lenny — something about missing product, likely just noise.

But the phone glitched. Froze. Then rebooted.

When it came back up, the inbox flashed:

NEW VOICEMAIL: #44

Duration: 00:57

The number was listed as PRIVATE.

Date: No data.

Ermi frowned. That voicemail box had been empty for months.

He played it.

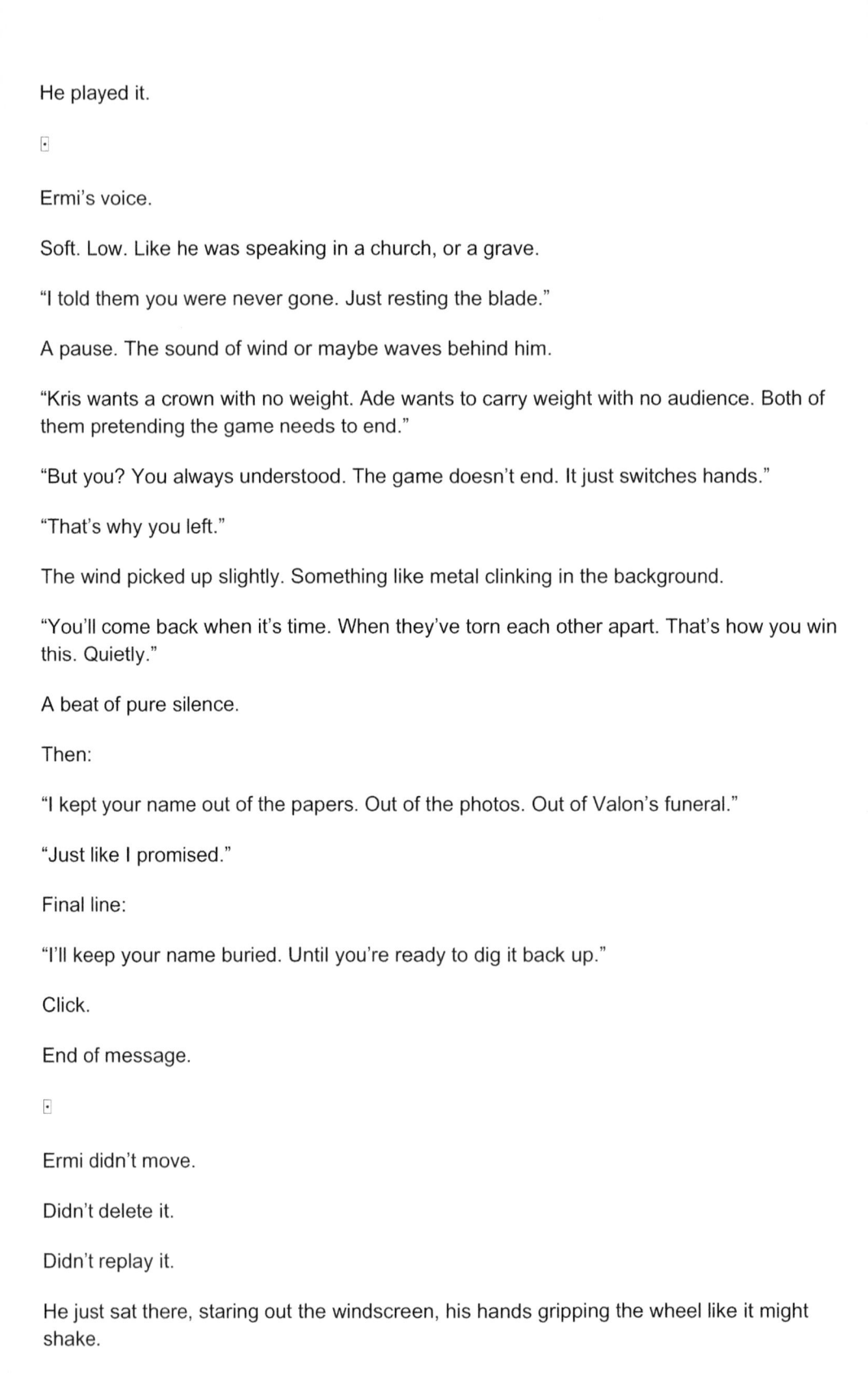

Ermi's voice.

Soft. Low. Like he was speaking in a church, or a grave.

"I told them you were never gone. Just resting the blade."

A pause. The sound of wind or maybe waves behind him.

"Kris wants a crown with no weight. Ade wants to carry weight with no audience. Both of them pretending the game needs to end."

"But you? You always understood. The game doesn't end. It just switches hands."

"That's why you left."

The wind picked up slightly. Something like metal clinking in the background.

"You'll come back when it's time. When they've torn each other apart. That's how you win this. Quietly."

A beat of pure silence.

Then:

"I kept your name out of the papers. Out of the photos. Out of Valon's funeral."

"Just like I promised."

Final line:

"I'll keep your name buried. Until you're ready to dig it back up."

Click.

End of message.

Ermi didn't move.

Didn't delete it.

Didn't replay it.

He just sat there, staring out the windscreen, his hands gripping the wheel like it might shake.

Then he whispered, to no one:

"They're going to find you."

And this time…

He didn't sound relieved.

It was left in the stairwell.

A manila folder, slid under the fourth-floor fire door of Maya's building. No envelope. No return. No markings except a single sticker on the flap:

FINAL PIECES

She brought it inside like it was radioactive. Sat at the kitchen table. Cleared everything else off.

Then opened it.

Inside:

- One photocopy of a Metropolitan Police internal report, watermarked but unfiled
- A printed spreadsheet — rows of names, dates, locations
- And a handwritten note on the back of a betting slip:

"You're not the first to ask. But you might be the last."

⸺

She scanned the report first.

Old-school, pre-digitisation. No metadata. The title:

"Persons of Persistent Interest — Marku Circuit (2005–2010)"

She didn't recognize half the names.

Dealers. Runners. Trainers. Three crooked lawyers. Two journalists. A mortician.

She started ticking through the "Status" column.

Dead

Missing

Presumed Deceased

Body Never Recovered

Over and over.

Until she hit the last three:

- Kristian Marku — "Active. Monitored. Last seen 48h ago."
- Ade Marku — "Known associate. No warrants. Believed armed."
- Levan — (no surname) — "Undeclared. Untagged. Unconfirmed. Possibly ghost."

Beside Levan's name, someone had scribbled a note in red pen:

"Ermi's wildcard? Or Valon's failsafe?"

Maya sat back.

There it was.

All of it.

This wasn't a story about two brothers.

It never had been.

This was about one ghost.

Still breathing.

And two men standing on either side of a flame that never went out — just passed hands.

She took a photo of the file. Backed it up. Twice. Then hid the folder inside the ceiling vent behind her bookshelf, wrapped in aluminium foil.

Not for safety.

For delay.

Someone had eyes on this.

And they wanted her to know just enough.

In the corner of the document, one last thing caught her eye:

A scribbled word.

No signature.

Just a single line written in hurried ink.

"Tick, tick, tick…"

Chapter 11 - Burn Notice

The barbershop was closed.

But the backroom was alive.

No mirrors. No razors. Just the soft, insect-whine hum of four desktop towers chained together under a folding table. A rack of drives blinking like nervous pupils. Wi-Fi routers, CD burners, encrypted NAS units stacked like Jenga blocks between hair dye boxes and bleach kits.

This wasn't a shop. It was a vault. The digital kind.

Photos. Messages. Surveillance footage. Court transcripts never filed. Fight contracts. Bribe ledgers. Even grainy phone vids from the night Valon died — backups of the backups. All stored here.

All about to burn.

⸻

Three men worked in silence, gloves on, phones in a Faraday pouch.

The oldest — Kav, square-shouldered, neck tattoo curling under his collar — supervised. The other two yanked drives from their ports and slammed them into a duffel bag like organs stolen from a body.

A fourth man — Juney, twenty-one, mouthy, twitchy, too curious — was meant to help.

He hesitated.

Held one hard drive back.

Slipped it into the inside pocket of his North Face jacket.

Quiet.

Kav saw.

Didn't say a word.

⸻

They finished stripping the units.

Then came the acetone.

Soaked the desk.

The carpet.

The walls.

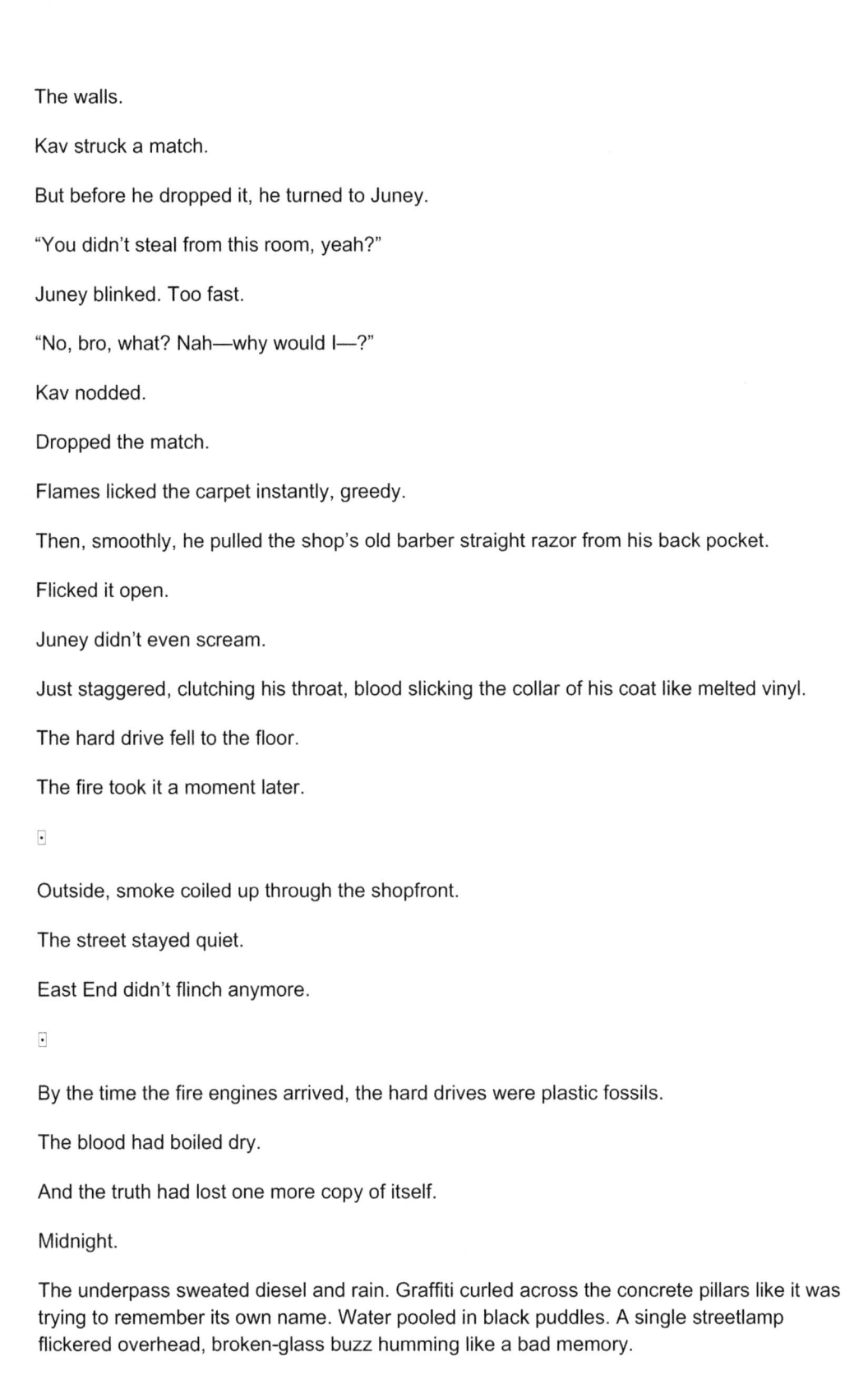

Kav struck a match.

But before he dropped it, he turned to Juney.

"You didn't steal from this room, yeah?"

Juney blinked. Too fast.

"No, bro, what? Nah—why would I—?"

Kav nodded.

Dropped the match.

Flames licked the carpet instantly, greedy.

Then, smoothly, he pulled the shop's old barber straight razor from his back pocket.

Flicked it open.

Juney didn't even scream.

Just staggered, clutching his throat, blood slicking the collar of his coat like melted vinyl.

The hard drive fell to the floor.

The fire took it a moment later.

Outside, smoke coiled up through the shopfront.

The street stayed quiet.

East End didn't flinch anymore.

By the time the fire engines arrived, the hard drives were plastic fossils.

The blood had boiled dry.

And the truth had lost one more copy of itself.

Midnight.

The underpass sweated diesel and rain. Graffiti curled across the concrete pillars like it was trying to remember its own name. Water pooled in black puddles. A single streetlamp flickered overhead, broken-glass buzz humming like a bad memory.

Ermi stood with his back to the pillar.

Smoking.

Waiting.

Then he heard the steps.

Boots on wet tarmac.

Deliberate.

He didn't look up.

"I was wondering when you'd stop pretending you didn't hear it."

Kris emerged from the shadows. Hood up. Fists already clenched.

"You sent it," he said.

Ermi took one last drag, then flicked the cigarette into the puddle.

"I didn't send shit," he said.

"But you recorded it."

Pause.

"You knew he was still alive."

Ermi nodded.

Kris took two steps forward.

"Why?" His voice cracked. "Why keep it quiet? Why bury him and parade us like—like fucking decoys?"

Ermi finally looked at him.

"You think this was about you?" he said softly. "You think Valon cared who looked best in front of the crowd?"

Kris's jaw flexed.

"You always hated me," he said. "You treated Ade like he was a blade, and me like a trophy."

"No," Ermi said. "I treated you like weight. Something that could break if dropped too hard."

He stepped closer.

"There were three of you."

Kris didn't move.

"Levan was first," Ermi said. "Came up quiet. Watched your dad bleed for the family. Watched me kill for it. And never asked to wear the crown. That's why Valon trusted him."

"Then why disappear him?" Kris snapped.

"He chose to disappear," Ermi said. "Because he knew if he stayed, you'd never be free. Neither of you. You'd always orbit his silence."

Kris's voice dropped. "Where is he?"

Ermi's mouth curled.

"Where you should have been."

Kris lunged — fast, shoulders tense, fist cocked — but Ermi didn't flinch.

The punch stopped an inch from his throat.

They stood like that.

Old blood vibrating between them.

Ermi whispered:

"You want to find him, you better pray he wants to be found."

He stepped back into the dark.

The streetlamp flickered once, then died.

⸱

Kris stayed there. Alone.

The silence screamed.

Not because he'd been lied to.

But because he'd finally started to believe it.

The dock smelled like steel regret.

Salt. Oil. Rotted wood. Tide-slapped silence.

Ade parked where the gravel thinned out and walked the last fifty feet to the caravan. It leaned like it was sick, roof dented, one window blacked out with duct tape.

No movement.

But the dog was gone.

He remembered the dog — big, wired, barked like a belt sander. It wasn't there.

He drew the gun from his waistband. Didn't raise it. Just kept it low. Casual. Necessary.

The caravan door creaked open with one push.

Inside: quiet.

One table. One microwave. A pile of dirty clothes. A TV from the 90s flashing blue screen.

And the smell.

Copper and meat.

He found the body half-buried behind the caravan.

Shallow dirt. A boot sticking out.

Matko Drini. Valon's sometime mechanic. A low-level ghost who was never important enough to fear — until he started talking.

Two shots to the chest. Close-range.

The hole hadn't been finished.

Whoever did this left in a rush — or didn't care about the funeral.

Ade knelt beside the body.

No wallet.

No phone.

But in the dirt, tucked beneath a paving stone:

A key.

Black plastic cap. No tag. Ordinary.

He went back inside. Checked the drawers. Cupboards. A single locked footlocker under the bed.

The key fit.

Inside:

Just one thing.

A photograph.

Glossy.

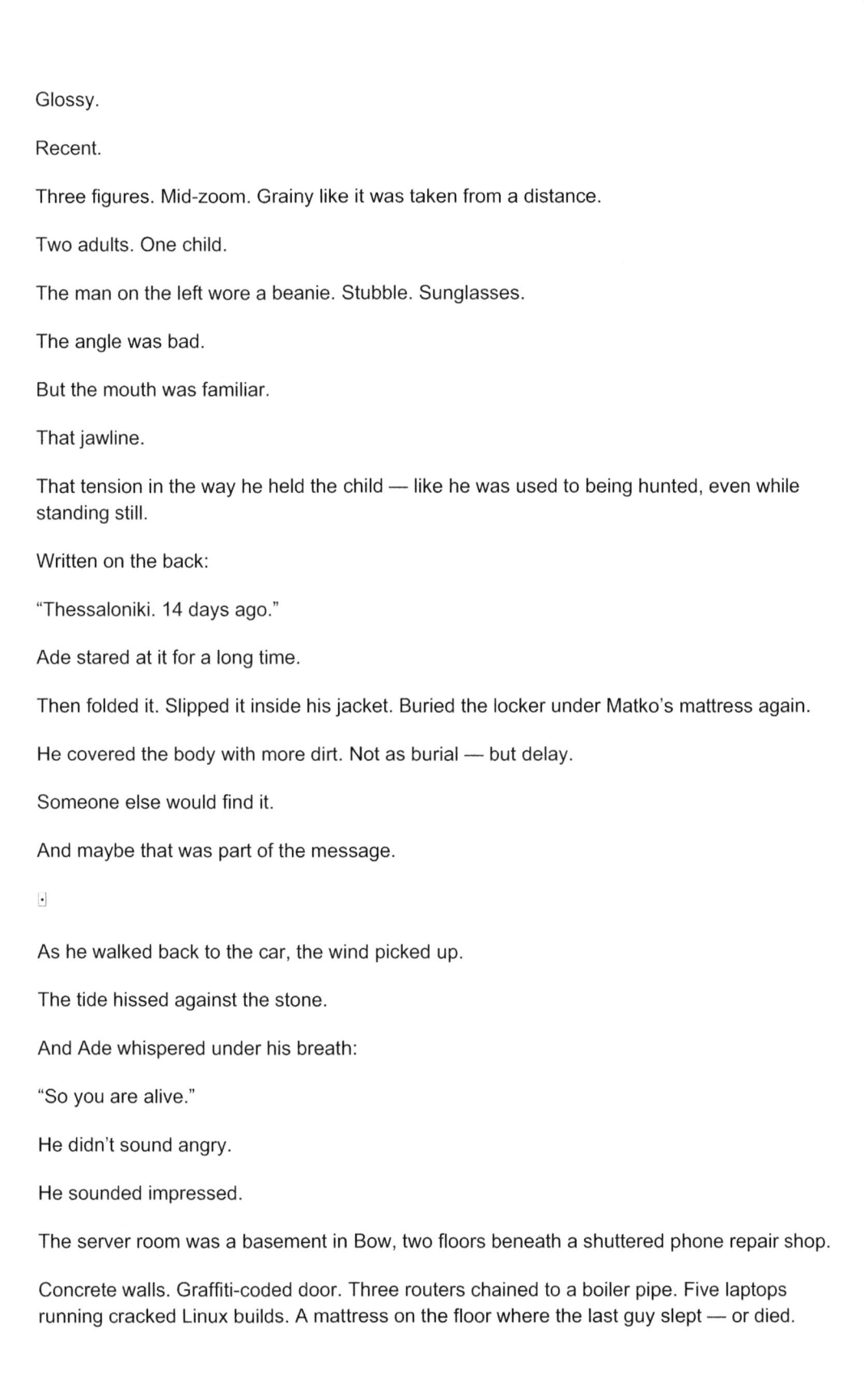

Recent.

Three figures. Mid-zoom. Grainy like it was taken from a distance.

Two adults. One child.

The man on the left wore a beanie. Stubble. Sunglasses.

The angle was bad.

But the mouth was familiar.

That jawline.

That tension in the way he held the child — like he was used to being hunted, even while standing still.

Written on the back:

"Thessaloniki. 14 days ago."

Ade stared at it for a long time.

Then folded it. Slipped it inside his jacket. Buried the locker under Matko's mattress again.

He covered the body with more dirt. Not as burial — but delay.

Someone else would find it.

And maybe that was part of the message.

⸱

As he walked back to the car, the wind picked up.

The tide hissed against the stone.

And Ade whispered under his breath:

"So you are alive."

He didn't sound angry.

He sounded impressed.

The server room was a basement in Bow, two floors beneath a shuttered phone repair shop.

Concrete walls. Graffiti-coded door. Three routers chained to a boiler pipe. Five laptops running cracked Linux builds. A mattress on the floor where the last guy slept — or died.

Maya wiped sweat from her neck, then keyed the mic.

Mic On. Stream Live.

The red light blinked.

She didn't start with a name.

Didn't start with a greeting.

She started with Valon's voice.

"If you're hearing this, you want truth. You want blood. You want to pin something to someone. Maybe both…"

She let it run twenty-three seconds — long enough to reach the line about "the one neither of them saw coming."

Then she cut the feed.

Switched to her own voice.

Calm. Focused. Edged like broken glass.

"You've heard the tapes. You know the names. But there was one he kept out of the fire. One who never got charged. Never got seen."

"He had keys to the kingdom before the others knew there was a door."

"His name is Levan."

She paused.

No script.

No notes.

Only facts.

"This isn't about justice. It's about direction. You want answers? Stop following the noise. Start following the silence."

Then:

"And if you're listening, Ermi…"

She leaned closer.

"…thanks for the voicemail."

She killed the stream.

Three minutes total.

Just enough.

Back upstairs, she packed her bag fast. Hard drive into one pouch. Gun into the other.

The building had no cameras.

But still — she felt watched.

As she stepped into the alley behind the shop, her burner buzzed.

UNKNOWN NUMBER. ONE MESSAGE.

"Now they'll come for you."

Maya stared at it.

Then, with a half-smile:

"Let them."

The smoke started just after 3 a.m.

Flat 6C — an unlisted unit in a derelict block off Devons Road — was already crumbling. No registered tenant. No electric meter. Squatters came and went, but no one stayed.

So when the top window popped with a soft blast and a coil of black smoke poured out like a curse, no one ran to help.

No one noticed — not until the flames were reflected in a puddle by the bus stop and someone called it in.

By 3:24 a.m., the fire brigade arrived.

By 3:33, they had it under control.

By 3:41, a body was recovered.

Burned beyond recognition.

The coroner couldn't pull prints. Dental was out — too much heat.

All they could confirm was male. Adult. Muscular build.

And the cause: accelerant-fueled ignition. Point of origin — sofa.

Intentional.

⸱

Detective Frey stood over the ruins of the living room, torchlight sweeping across the blistered walls.

"Anything left?" she asked the fire officer.

He nodded.

"Just this."

He handed her a small evidence bag.

Inside: a ring.

Thick. Black. Scorched.

But the engraving inside was untouched.

MARKU.

Frey didn't speak for a moment.

Then nodded.

"Leak it."

⸱

By 5 a.m., the press had it:

ONE DEAD IN EAST END FLAT BLAZE — MARKU RING RECOVERED

No names. No confirmations.

But the whispers spread fast.

"Was it Kris?"

"No way — Ade was the quiet one. Had to be him."

"Unless it was a fake."

"Unless it was Levan."

No one knew.

That was the trick.

Uncertainty was the loudest kind of control.

At 5:17 a.m., someone sent Maya a photo.

Just one.

The ring.

Then a message:

"Only one of them's coming back. Tick, tick."

Across the city, in two different places, Kris and Ade stared at the same headline — at the same time — not knowing if it was about them, or for them.

Neither moved.

Neither reached out.

The war had stopped pretending to wait.

Chapter 12 - Inheritance Teeth

The basement stank of ink, mildew, and forgotten crimes.

Fluorescent lights buzzed overhead like they were trying to remember how to hum. Filing cabinets lined the walls — dented metal, stickers peeled, corners warped by damp.

It wasn't a vault in the modern sense.

It was worse.

Paper.

Which meant intentional.

Kris kept the door closed behind him. The man seated at the desk — hunched, white-haired, wearing socks but no shoes — didn't meet his eye.

Petar Markovic.

Valon's accountant for twelve years. Never arrested. Never seen. Paid to remember quietly.

Kris stood in front of him like a judge who hated the robe.

"You know what I'm here for."

Petar nodded. His voice rasped like worn carpet.

"Cabinet four. Bottom drawer. Code is your birthday."

Kris didn't ask how he knew it.

He crossed the room, crouched, and spun the dial on the old rotary lock.

Click.

The drawer groaned as it slid open.

Inside:

- A small leather-bound notebook.
- A rolled blueprint of what looked like club floorplans.
- A red-covered ledger titled: "Unfiled — Interim."

Kris took the ledger.

Set it on the desk.

Opened it.

Names. Dozens. Cross-referenced with payments, dates, symbols he didn't recognize — Valon's code. Most names had been struck through.

One page in particular had no strike.

Just a name.

Levan.

Circled.

Next to it: three columns of figures — no payouts. No deductions. Just a location line:

Durrës, early pull.

And beside it, in red ink, not part of the columns:

"Clean fire. Quiet hands."

Kris stared.

"You knew," he said softly. "You always knew he wasn't just part of this."

Petar finally looked at him.

"He was the first version."

Kris blinked.

"What?"

"Valon never wanted a legacy," Petar said. "He wanted an echo. Something that couldn't be traced back."

"Then why raise me?"

"To distract everyone else," Petar said, his voice dry as bone. "He needed a sun for them to orbit. And a shadow for the work."

Kris closed the ledger.

"Where is he now?"

Petar shook his head.

"Never knew. I wasn't supposed to."

Kris looked at the notebook. Didn't touch it.

Then turned.

Walked out without a word.

Up the narrow stairs, into the cold light of late morning, Kris stepped into the alley and breathed deep.

Not relief.

Recognition.

He wasn't left behind.

He was built for bait.

And now?

He wasn't playing that role anymore.

The club's back office stank of old champagne and cheap carpet glue.

The music from the floor pounded through the walls like a second heartbeat — bass-heavy, constant, disinterested in anything human.

Lenny sat in the single leather chair like it was a throne.

Across from him: Kojo, young, cocky, dressed like an influencer with too many sponsors and not enough instincts.

He was sweating through his collar.

Beside him stood Baz and Uka — Lenny's long-time problem-solvers. One held a rag. The other held a knife. Neither looked in a hurry.

Lenny rolled up his sleeves.

His shirt was spotless.

"Where'd you hear it?" he asked.

Kojo shook his head. "Didn't. Swear. Just heard whispers. Some girl on a stream—"

"You repeated it," Lenny interrupted.

"It was nothing!"

Lenny held up one hand.

"'Levan,' right?"

Kojo flinched.

"Some name from nowhere. Said he was alive. Some old man's ghost."

Lenny stood.

"You know why I'm angry, Kojo?"

Kojo swallowed.

"Because I told the wrong people?"

"No."

Lenny smiled — small, sharp.

"Because you remembered the wrong story."

Kojo blinked. "What—?"

Lenny stepped close. Took the knife from Uka without looking.

"Valon built a myth. Then burned the real version. We don't resurrect myths. We bury them deeper."

And before Kojo could speak again—

Lenny dragged the knife across his cheek.

Slow. Not deep. But final.

Kojo screamed, jerking back, blood spilling like red ink.

Lenny didn't blink.

"You talk again, I take your tongue."

He handed the knife back.

Nodded to Baz.

"Clean it. Stitch it. Then drop him in Barking with a hoodie and no wallet."

He turned back to his desk.

Picked up his drink. Sipped.

Then said, without turning around:

"If I hear that name again from anyone in this room, I start using teeth."

·

In the corner, an old CRT monitor blinked. Security feed.

One figure watched from the top-right screen.

Blurry. Hooded. Standing outside the club, unmoving.

Watching.

Not Kojo.

Not Maya.

Not Kris.

Not Ade.

Just waiting.

Maya sat in the archives room of a shuttered immigration consultancy in Harlesden, lit only by a halogen desk lamp and the white glow of a battered Lenovo laptop. The walls were lined with metal filing cabinets, each drawer tagged with years no one wanted to remember.

She was knee-deep in forgeries.

Old-school stuff. Pre-Brexit era. Black ink and blue stamps. Bad lamination.

That was where she found it.

⸱

A scanned copy of a 1996 Albanian passport.

Name: Ardit M. Cela

Date of birth: approximate

Issued: Durrës

Status: REVOKED

Forgery tag: "Style 4.3 – internal/constructed alias, non-extraditable"

The photo was unmistakable.

Levan.

Older than the last sighting. Sharper jawline. Hollowed cheeks. Eyes that didn't look at the camera — they assessed it. Like he was seeing through the lens to the man holding it.

But the real kicker wasn't the name.

It was the family field.

Listed under "Dependent":

Cela, Drin M.

Age: 7. Male. Born in Greece.

And an ID stub code.

Not in Albania.

Croydon.

Three months ago.

⁌

Maya sat back.

Her heart didn't race. It slowed.

This wasn't flight anymore.

This was fortification.

Levan wasn't hiding in the shadows like a fugitive.

He was carving a space for something he built.

A child.

A shadow's shadow.

⁌

She printed two copies. One stayed in her coat. One in a dead-letter box she'd rented months ago under an alias no one had reason to watch.

Then she turned off the light, packed up, and left through the back door.

The air outside was sharp. Wet. Charged.

She pulled her phone.

Texted a number labeled only: HUNTER

Croydon. Child. Name: Drin. We move quiet. No alarm.

If Levan's watching — he'll come to him. Not us.

No reply.

Didn't need one.

⁌

Down the street, an unmarked car's dome light clicked on.

Not police.

Not friends.

Just interested parties.

The church smelled like plaster dust and wood oil.

Bare beams overhead. Scaffold spine running up one wall. No pews. No cross. Just concrete benches and sun leaking in through boarded windows. The altar was still raw stone, wrapped in plastic like it might infect someone.

Kris stepped in first.

Boots loud on the half-tiled floor. Jacket unzipped. No weapon visible.

Ade waited by the half-built pulpit. Hands in his coat pockets. Still. Watching.

For a long beat, neither said anything.

Then Kris stopped ten feet away.

"How'd you know I'd come?"

Ade didn't look away.

"You're still angry enough to believe you can fix it."

Kris sniffed, once. Half a laugh. Half something darker.

"You really think he's alive."

"I know it."

Kris stepped closer.

"And you're just fine with that?"

"No," Ade said. "I'm just done pretending he wasn't part of this."

Kris circled slowly, eyes on the beams.

"I thought we were the legacy," he said. "That everything he built—"

"—was built for him," Ade interrupted.

Kris didn't answer.

They stood in silence again.

The sound of hammers echoed faintly from outside. Far off. Not close enough to interrupt.

Ade took out a folded paper. Set it on the stone altar.

Kris approached.

It was the photo — the one Maya had released. The grainy passport. The child.

"He's not hiding," Ade said. "He's waiting."

Kris stared at the image.

"That's what scares me."

Ade nodded.

"He didn't want the crown. He wanted the quiet. He always did."

Another pause.

Then Kris said, quietly:

"If he's alive… it's because we weren't enough."

Ade looked at him.

Not in anger.

In agreement.

"We still aren't."

⸱

A long silence.

Then Kris turned to leave.

But before stepping out of the shadowed doorway, he said:

"If I see him before you do…"

Ade nodded once.

"Don't try to finish what Valon started."

⸱

The door closed behind him.

Dust rose.

And the empty altar waited.

The safehouse sat at the edge of a farm road, faceless and forgotten.

No address. No mailbox. The windows were frosted. The grass outside uncut.

Inside: one bed, one fridge, no family photos.

And a boy.

No older than seven.

Skin olive-tinted. Hair cropped short. Eyes too large for his frame — sharp, quiet, waiting.

He sat cross-legged on a floor rug, playing with a piece of leather. A wrist strap. Faded black. On it, three brass letters hammered in:

D. M. L.

He ran his fingers across the L slowly, like he knew what it stood for, even if no one had ever said it aloud.

The room was silent except for the fridge's low whirr.

On the table beside him: a burner phone. Old, plastic, no screen light.

Then—

It rang.

One single vibration.

He didn't flinch.

Just reached. Picked it up. Pressed it to his ear.

No hello.

No words.

Just breathing.

Then a voice.

Faint.

Filtered through static and sea air.

Masculine. Familiar.

"It's time."

Click.

Call ended.

The boy stood.

Picked up the strap. Fastened it around his wrist with slow, practiced fingers.

Walked to the front door.

Opened it.

Stepped out into the cold.

Far off, an engine idled.

Headlights off.

Just waiting.

Chapter 13 - Names We Dont Bury

The lab was disguised as a radiator repair shop.

Peeling red signage. Rusted lockbox. Four mismatched chairs in the lobby with dust patterns where asses used to be.

But behind the false panel in the supply closet: the real room. No windows. Low ceiling. Four computers. One laminator. A tray of dyes and signature stencils. Fluorescent light so sharp it seemed to buzz inside your skull.

At the desk: Rami — ex-intelligence, now freelance. Bulgarian passport, Israeli pistol, Serbian cigarettes. His fingers worked fast. Efficient. Unnervous.

In front of him lay three documents.

All unfinished.

All for the same person.

A child.

⸫

First: School record. Name: Drin Cela.

Second: Birth certificate. Albania to Greece, naturalised via "private sponsor."

Third: Passport. New name: Kreshnik Cela. Nationality: Irish.

Rami adjusted the birth year. Tweaked the signature line.

On the margin of the form, he wrote a note to himself:

Kreshnik = "the chosen" or "hero."

He didn't ask questions.

Not until he looked at the payment envelope.

Cash. Clean. New euros, all banded.

And tucked inside: a reference card.

Client contact: E. M.

He flipped it over.

And there it was, in faint pencil — just two letters. Almost a whisper.

"Er."

Rami leaned back in his chair.

That name meant London.

That name meant heat.

He didn't like heat.

But he also didn't say no.

He pulled a burner phone from the drawer. Opened Signal. Sent one message.

Kreshnik file complete. Collection 48h. Notify E. M. only. No third party.

He tucked the passport-in-progress into a heat-sealed envelope.

Stamped the wax.

Then lit a cigarette — not out of stress.

Out of ritual.

Whenever he made a new name…

He always burned the first one.

And in the waste tray, already turned to ash:

Cela, Drin M.

The man opened the door with a limp and a revolver.

He didn't aim it.

Just held it loose by his thigh, like arthritis had taken all the fear out of him.

Maya raised both hands.

"Not here to collect," she said. "Here to remember."

The man squinted.

A long moment passed.

Then he stepped aside.

Inside, the flat smelled like boiled coffee and hospital soap. Cracked linoleum. Blackout curtains. A radio playing news in another language — Albanian, maybe — with the volume low, like memory had volume too.

He poured two mugs. One sugar cube. No milk.

Set them down.

"You know my name?" he asked.

"Only what you left behind," Maya said. "False ones. Rotating bank cards. A few photos that never had dates."

"Then you don't know shit."

"I know you vanished," she said. "Right before Valon died."

"Everyone vanished after Valon died."

"Not like you."

She reached into her coat.

Slid a photo across the table.

Three men. Blurred. Taken in the '90s. One of them was him — younger, sharper, holding a burner and standing beside a body in a canal.

The second man was unrecognizable. Just a figure in the dark.

The third was Levan.

Not a child.

A shadow.

The man across from her looked down at it for a long time.

Then he said:

"He told me to run before the order came."

Maya didn't blink.

"Valon gave the order to kill you?"

He nodded.

"But Levan warned you?"

Another nod.

"Why?"

The man sipped his coffee. The cube had barely dissolved.

"Because I took his photo."

Pause.

"Not many did."

She leaned forward.

"You worked for Valon. But you listened to Levan."

"I listened to the one who didn't speak in front of mirrors."

Silence.

Then, softly, Maya asked:

"Was he trying to save you?"

The old man smiled — cracked and sad.

"No. He was trying to save the world from turning into your story."

⸺

Maya left with the photo.

And a name she hadn't heard in years.

"Drinian."

The man had whispered it as she walked out.

Not like a name.

Like a password.

The flat was silent in that preserved kind of way — not forgotten, but protected.

Kris stepped in slow. No lights. Just the weak morning grey creeping through a split in the curtains. Dust hung midair like suspended ash. The doorknob had felt untouched. No drag marks. No signs of break-ins.

But he knew it was his.

Levan's.

No one else would've left the blinds half open, facing east — just enough to know what time it was, never enough to see what was coming.

The layout was surgical.

A single bed. No sheets.

A chair with the cushion gutted and restuffed with cash.

And a steel lockbox, bolted to the floor under the table leg.

Kris pulled it free. No hesitation.

Code?

Not needed.

He already knew the pattern — a number Levan used on gym lockers twenty years ago:

1-4-6-9.

Click.

The lid lifted.

Inside:

Six slim black journals, bound with thread. Unlabeled.

No dates. No titles.

Just content — scrawled in tight columns, some lines blacked out with marker. Others rewritten underneath in pencil. A few pages written entirely upside down.

Kris flipped through.

First entry he found:

"Ade thinks fear earns respect. But it earns silence. Same shape. Different echo."

Another:

"Kris is all forward motion. No brakes. You need someone to build a wall. Not a fire."

He stopped cold at the next.

A name.

"Drinian – held in pocket for when silence stops being enough."

Another page. Near the middle.

This one boxed in ink.

The only boxed one.

"If they find the boy, they'll come for each other. Let them."

Kris froze.

His reflection in the window was barely visible. Just a shape. A possibility.

He sat in the chair.

Kept flipping.

On the final page, in faint red ink — almost faded:

"I'm not gone. I'm just elsewhere. Watch how they behave without a script."

The page below was torn out.

He stared at the jagged edge.

Then closed the book.

No anger.

No panic.

Just one thought — sharp as a needle, sinking in:

He planned this. All of it.

The butcher shop had been closed for four years, but Lenny kept the back room cold.

The light flickered overhead, rhythmic like a timer winding down.

Ade didn't knock.

He stepped inside, past the broken freezer, past the hanging chains that used to hold beef and now held silence.

Lenny was already sitting at the stainless steel table.

No guards. No weapon visible. Just a glass of water and a thick ring of keys that didn't match any doors in this building.

"A drink?" Lenny offered.

Ade shut the door behind him.

"You lit 6C."

Not a question.

Lenny nodded once.

"Wasn't personal."

Ade stepped closer.

"Then what was it?"

Lenny looked up.

"You let a myth grow long enough, it eats the truth."

"You killed someone to make a point?"

Lenny snorted. "Someone was already dead. I just chose the venue."

Ade's jaw clenched.

"You think you're in control of this?"

"I know what I'm not doing," Lenny said. "Chasing ghosts. Bending my knees every time someone whispers Levan like it's a church name."

He sipped his water.

"I burn things to remind people who's real."

Ade didn't move.

"And what happens when the myth burns back?"

Lenny leaned forward.

"That's the trick, Ade. It won't."

A pause.

Then, almost softly:

"He won't."

Silence stretched between them. Long and taut.

Lenny tapped the chair opposite.

"Sit down."

Ade didn't.

"I'm not staying."

Lenny's eyes narrowed.

"You came all this way just to threaten me?"

"No," Ade said. "I came to see if you flinched."

Lenny grinned.

"Did I?"

Ade's eyes flicked to the keys.

"No."

Then he walked out.

No nod.

No warning.

Just departure.

⸱

Behind him, Lenny stayed seated.

But his grin slipped — just enough to reveal the quiet behind his teeth.

Maya sat alone in the cheap rental flat in Vauxhall, high above the river where the wind never stopped screaming against the glass.

In front of her: Levan's first forged passport.

She'd looked at it a dozen times.

She hadn't seen the message.

Until now.

⸱

On the back of the photograph, behind the lamination, faint and curling like it had been scratched in with the point of a pin, were nine words — a line, barely visible:

"Kur të zhduken yjet, ai do të zgjohet."

She whispered it aloud.

Then again, slower.

Her mother used to sing it, during blackouts. When the power went out in Tirana and the whole city felt like it might slide off the edge of history.

"When the stars disappear… he will wake."

It wasn't poetry.

It was instruction.

And the next line — the one Levan didn't write, but Maya remembered — was the name:

"Drinian."

She closed her eyes.

He'd used it in the story he told — Valon too. A tale they made up for the boys when they were kids. About a boy who lived under a mountain until the sky cracked. Not a hero. Just a survivor.

A name no one outside the family ever heard.

Until now.

⸺

Maya picked up the file from Sofia. The new identity.

Kreshnik Cela.

It was clever.

Kreshnik meant hero.

But Levan never gave him that name.

He named him for endurance.

Drinian wasn't meant to rule.

He was meant to outlast.

⸺

On her burner, Maya typed a note to herself. Not to send. Just to remember:

"He didn't name the boy after a legacy. He named him after a future."

⸺

Behind her, a low beeping started.

One of her motion alerts.

Not a breach.

Just a presence.

Someone standing still at the edge of the hallway camera.

Not moving.

Not entering.

Just being seen.

She didn't check the feed.

She didn't need to.

Chapter 14 - A Mouthful of Matches

The chapel was rented by the hour.

Bare stone, cold wood. No name carved into the marble at the altar. No urn on the pedestal. Just a sealed black box filled with something burned and human.

Kris stood alone at the front.

No clergy.

No candles.

No script.

Just the sound of the rain hitting the roof — fast, relentless, uncaring.

He wore no black.

Just the same coat he'd worn when he thought Ade might shoot him. Or hug him. Or both.

.

He cleared his throat.

No one to hear it.

Still, he spoke.

"I don't know if this is for my brother… or the piece of me that still thought any of this ended clean."

His voice didn't shake. It landed like gravel thrown at a windshield.

"If it's Ade in that box, then the last thing I said to him was a warning. If it's someone else… then the warning's still good."

He looked down at his own hands. Scarred. Still. Capable.

"We used to think family was what stood behind you in a fight. But sometimes, it's the thing that waits for you to fall, just so it can carry your name forward and call it grief."

He walked to the box.

Rested one hand on it.

"You always said you'd die before they got to you. So either you were wrong… or this is just another move."

He stepped back.

Looked at the empty seats. Thought about what it meant to bury something without knowing what you'd buried.

Then:

"If this is the last time I say your name, Ade… I'll make sure it cuts."

He turned. Walked out.

Left the box behind.

Didn't look back.

⸱

Across the city, in a parking garage two levels underground, a man sat in a car with the chapel's audio streaming through his speakers.

Not live. Not hacked.

Invited.

He listened to the last words.

Then muted it.

He smiled.

And whispered, just once:

"Good. Let him feel it."

The observation room was white, windowless, and cold.

One steel chair. One table. One pane of reinforced glass — two-way, but the light on Maya's side made sure the boy couldn't see her clearly.

Unless he already knew where to look.

⸱

Drin sat on the other side.

Seven years old.

Brown jumper. Grey tracksuit bottoms. Clean sneakers. Clean everything.

Except his eyes.

They didn't belong to a child.

He didn't fidget.

Didn't blink often.

Didn't speak.

Just stared straight ahead, arms crossed on the table, mouth pressed into a line like he was biting a secret.

Maya leaned forward, close to the mic.

"Drin. My name is Maya Khan. I'm not police. I'm not here to scare you."

No response.

"I just want to talk. To understand. You're safe here. No one's going to hurt you."

Still nothing.

She pressed the mic again.

"Do you know why you're here?"

Drin moved — a slight tilt of the head. Then, finally, a sentence. Measured. Memorised.

"He told me not to talk to you."

Maya's breath caught.

"He — Levan?"

No answer.

"Is he your father?"

A pause.

Then:

"He said your voice sounds like someone who's trying to remember what betrayal feels like."

The words didn't sound like they belonged to a child. They were delivered — not spoken. Recited.

Maya stared at him through the glass.

He didn't look scared.

He looked trained.

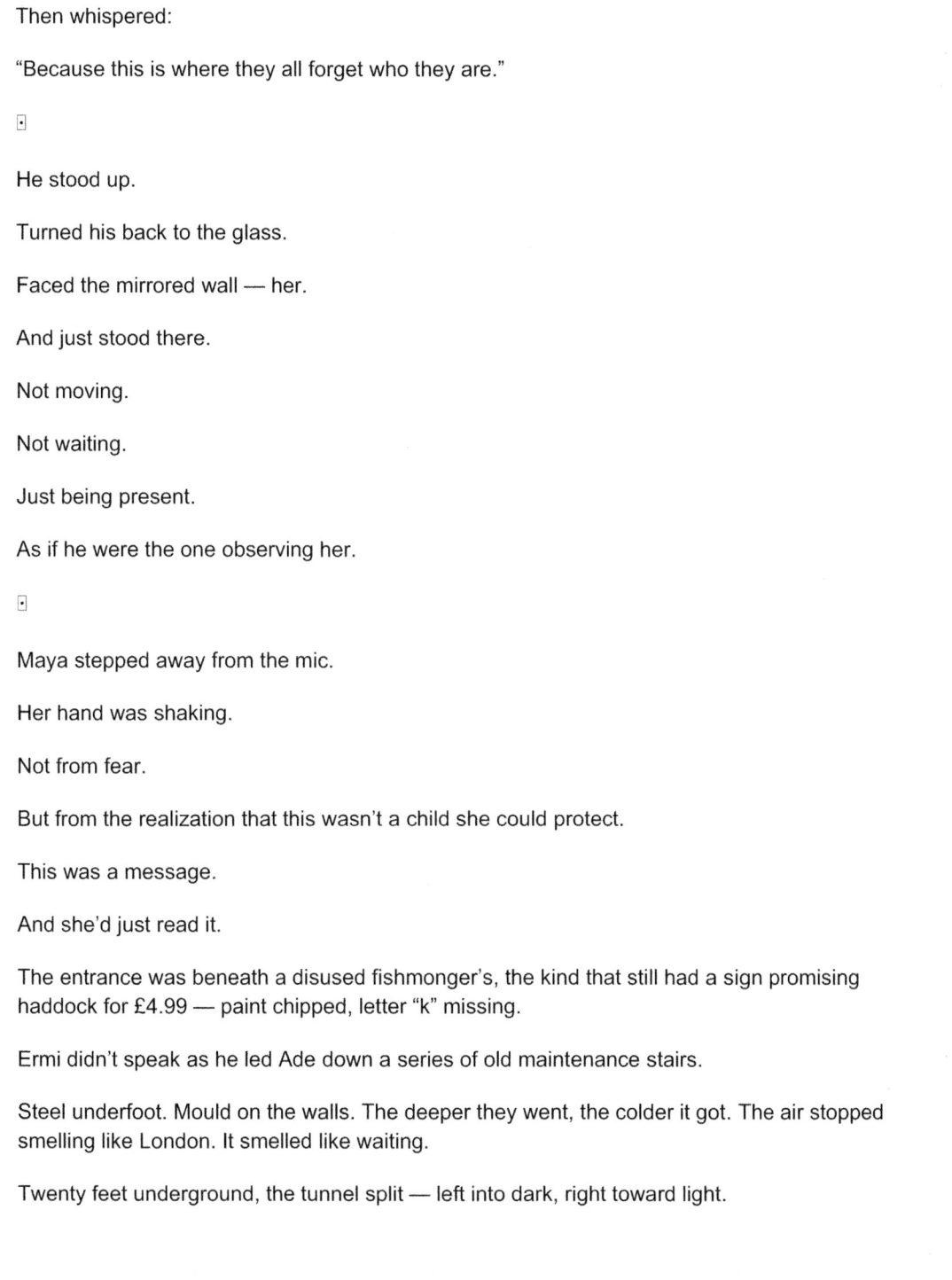

She tapped the mic once more, softly.

"Why did he bring you here?"

Drin blinked, just once.

Then whispered:

"Because this is where they all forget who they are."

⸭

He stood up.

Turned his back to the glass.

Faced the mirrored wall — her.

And just stood there.

Not moving.

Not waiting.

Just being present.

As if he were the one observing her.

⸭

Maya stepped away from the mic.

Her hand was shaking.

Not from fear.

But from the realization that this wasn't a child she could protect.

This was a message.

And she'd just read it.

The entrance was beneath a disused fishmonger's, the kind that still had a sign promising haddock for £4.99 — paint chipped, letter "k" missing.

Ermi didn't speak as he led Ade down a series of old maintenance stairs.

Steel underfoot. Mould on the walls. The deeper they went, the colder it got. The air stopped smelling like London. It smelled like waiting.

Twenty feet underground, the tunnel split — left into dark, right toward light.

Ermi took the right.

Ade followed, silent.

The corridor opened into a vast concrete cavity, low-ceilinged and stale. There were broken roulette tables, a collapsed blackjack pit, and a half-burned sign:

"RED ROOM CASINO."

It had been buried for at least a decade.

Only one table remained standing — a poker table under a single bulb.

At it sat a man.

Black leather coat. Pale hands. Face like a faded photo: clean, quiet, made of angles.

He didn't stand.

He simply said:

"So this is Valon's unfinished knife."

Ade didn't reply.

He looked at Ermi.

Ermi said nothing.

Didn't move.

Didn't even blink.

The seated man gestured to the chair opposite.

Ade didn't sit.

The man nodded, unsurprised.

"You don't know my name. But you know my work."

Ade's tone was flat.

"I know ghosts don't bleed."

"That's where you're wrong," the man said. "Ghosts bleed, they just do it in other people's names."

He lifted a stack of old Polaroids from the table.

Spread them like cards.

People. Dead ones.

Burned. Shot. Gone.

Ade didn't look down.

"What is this?"

"Proof that the war started long before you picked up a gun."

"Whose side were you on?"

The man smiled.

"There are no sides. Only survivors and authors."

He pushed one photo forward — face-down.

Ade flipped it.

It was Levan.

But not recently.

This was fifteen years ago.

Blood on his collar.

Gun in his hand.

A boy — maybe twelve — standing behind him. Watching.

It wasn't Kris.

It wasn't Ade.

"Who's the kid?"

"That's what you're here to find out," the man said. "You thought Levan stepped out of the story. He didn't."

"He started a new one."

⸻

Ade took the photo.

Didn't thank him.

Just turned and walked out.

Behind him, Ermi didn't follow.

He stayed at the table.

Sat down.

And whispered to the man:

"It's almost time."

The man smiled.

"It's past time."

Lenny hated unanswered questions.

Especially when they took the shape of a man like Baz — six-foot-four, neck like a pillar, arms that had held more dying men than most morticians.

Gone.

Not dead.

Gone.

No struggle. No note. No threats.

Just absence.

⸱

Lenny stood in the hallway of Baz's flat — top floor, Brixton, steel-reinforced locks, two cameras disabled at once.

Inside, the place was untouched.

Bed made.

Fridge stocked.

Gun safe open — empty.

No shell casings. No mess.

Just a burner phone left neatly on the kitchen counter. Not Baz's usual. A cheap one.

Lenny picked it up. No pin. One message waiting. Audio file. No label.

He hit play.

⸱

"You taught him to kill."

Levan's voice.

No doubt. No disguise. Calm as a held breath.

"You taught him to clean. To erase. To forget."

"But you never taught him to question. That's why he left you."

A pause. Then:

"The fire doesn't come for liars, Lenny. It comes for those who believe them."

Click.

Silence.

⸺

Lenny gripped the phone tight.

Not from rage.

But from something worse.

Recognition.

Baz hadn't run.

He'd chosen.

⸺

In the corner of the room, on the table near the window, Baz had left his jacket. Inside it, the metal tag Lenny gave all his inner circle — name, date, loyalty code.

Baz had scratched a single line into the metal.

Not words.

Just a symbol.

A flame.

⸺

Outside, on the street, a bus drove past with a flickering digital ad.

A face glitched onscreen for half a second — dark-eyed, sharp-jawed, gone too fast to catch.

But Lenny saw it.

And he knew.

It began with a hum — low, almost mechanical.

Then silence.

Then his voice.

No music. No signature. Just Levan.

Calm. Level. Spoken like scripture from a man who'd already been to hell and didn't need directions back.

"You've spent years building a version of events you could sleep beside."

"You put names on plaques, crimes on others, and innocence in the mouths of people who never earned it."

"You turned family into firewood."

A pause. Breath.

Then:

"But the boy is not part of your myth."

"He does not owe you forgiveness. Or fear."

"He does not carry the debts of my name."

Another pause. Just long enough to matter.

"If you chase the boy, you chase me."

"If you chase me, you chase the part of yourself you buried years ago — the part that whispered when you first pulled the trigger: This will come back."

The voice never cracked.

Never threatened.

It offered.

"Let the flame eat what it must."

"Or burn with it."

Click.

The message dropped on every backchannel at once.

Telegram. Burner Discords. Pirate radio. Airdrops to phones in Lenny's crew. On Maya's encrypted cloud. Into the inbox of a dead journalist's archived drive.

No metadata.

No source.

Just truth.

⸰

In an apartment above a Polish bakery, Kris played it twice.

Then lit a cigarette with the same lighter his uncle gave him the day Valon went underground.

Didn't speak.

Didn't move.

Just sat in the dark.

Listening.

⸰

On the south bank, under a bridge near the old wharf, Ade heard it on a handheld from a stranger who nodded and walked away without speaking.

He stood there for ten minutes after it ended.

Unblinking.

As if waiting for the voice to come back and say the real part.

⸰

And in a safehouse in a town with no name, a boy sat at a desk with headphones over his ears.

He didn't flinch at the sound.

Didn't cry.

He just whispered one word under his breath:

"Baba."

Then he reached for the switch on the lamp beside him. And turned it off

Chapter 15 - The car, The Flame, The Silence

The rooftop was quiet.

Mid-level office block in Stratford — once used for telecoms, now fenced off with rusted wire and tagged with teenage threats: names, hearts, half-spelled oaths.

Kris moved across the rooftop with one hand in his coat, the other carrying the parcel. Nothing bulky. Just a paperback-sized box. Taped once. No label.

Inside:

- A burner phone preloaded with one contact.
- A small brass key, worn down at the teeth.
- A folded map with a red mark on a derelict substation near the M25.
- A single photo. The boy. Not from Maya — from Levan's flat.

He set the package behind a ventilation duct.

Not under it. Not hidden.

Placed.

Like an offering.

He checked his watch.

Waited.

First ten minutes: he paced.

Twenty: stood still.

Thirty: crouched and lit a cigarette.

He didn't feel nervous. Not exactly.

But something about the wind made the rooftop feel… thinner. Like he could fall through it without falling off it.

The kind of stillness where something is about to move.

After an hour, he stood.

Looked once around.

Then again, slower.

The city stretched below, unconcerned.

He said, aloud:

"Alright, Ade. Say something."

No answer.

⸺

He walked back to the parcel.

Took one last look at the map inside.

Then turned away.

Didn't pick it up.

Didn't destroy it.

Left it.

For who?

He didn't know anymore.

But someone would come.

⸺

Back on the street, as he slid into a black car with no plates, he looked once into the rearview mirror.

No one behind him.

Still — he didn't blink.

Didn't relax.

The driver asked, "Straight there?"

Kris said:

"No. Make them think we turned back. Then go."

The driver nodded.

Pulled away.

Two rooftops over, a figure stood still against a water tank.

Watching.

Holding a phone.

Pressing record.

Queen's Cross Hospital had long since abandoned its parking structure to private security and public decay.

Cameras worked — but not well.

Signage was still bright — but the paint peeled on everything else.

Bay 12B sat near the top floor, half-covered by a concrete overhang.

Shadowed.

Unmonitored.

Perfect.

⸻

The car was already there.

Black BMW, windows tinted too dark for legal use.

Engine off.

Doors unlocked.

Kris arrived first.

Didn't rush. Didn't check the surroundings.

He opened the rear driver-side door and slid in without a word.

Settled back. Hands on his knees. Jaw locked.

He didn't look at the empty seat next to him.

He knew.

⸻

Seven minutes later, footsteps echoed from the stairwell.

Not fast.

Not hesitant.

Just certain.

Ade appeared in the doorway. No coat. No bag. Just a phone in his pocket and a print of a photo folded once in his hand.

He didn't hesitate.

Opened the rear passenger door and stepped in.

Closed it.

Sat.

Didn't speak.

Didn't look at Kris.

⸱

They sat in silence.

Not awkward.

Not angry.

Just quiet.

The kind that wraps around two people who already know the shape of the argument they won't have.

Outside the car, pigeons scratched near the barriers.

A breeze pushed dust along the concrete.

Somewhere below, a car alarm chirped and fell silent.

⸱

Kris finally reached into his coat.

Pulled out the lighter.

Held it in his palm like it might answer a question for him.

He didn't flick it.

He just said:

"Do you think he knew it'd end like this?"

Ade didn't look over.

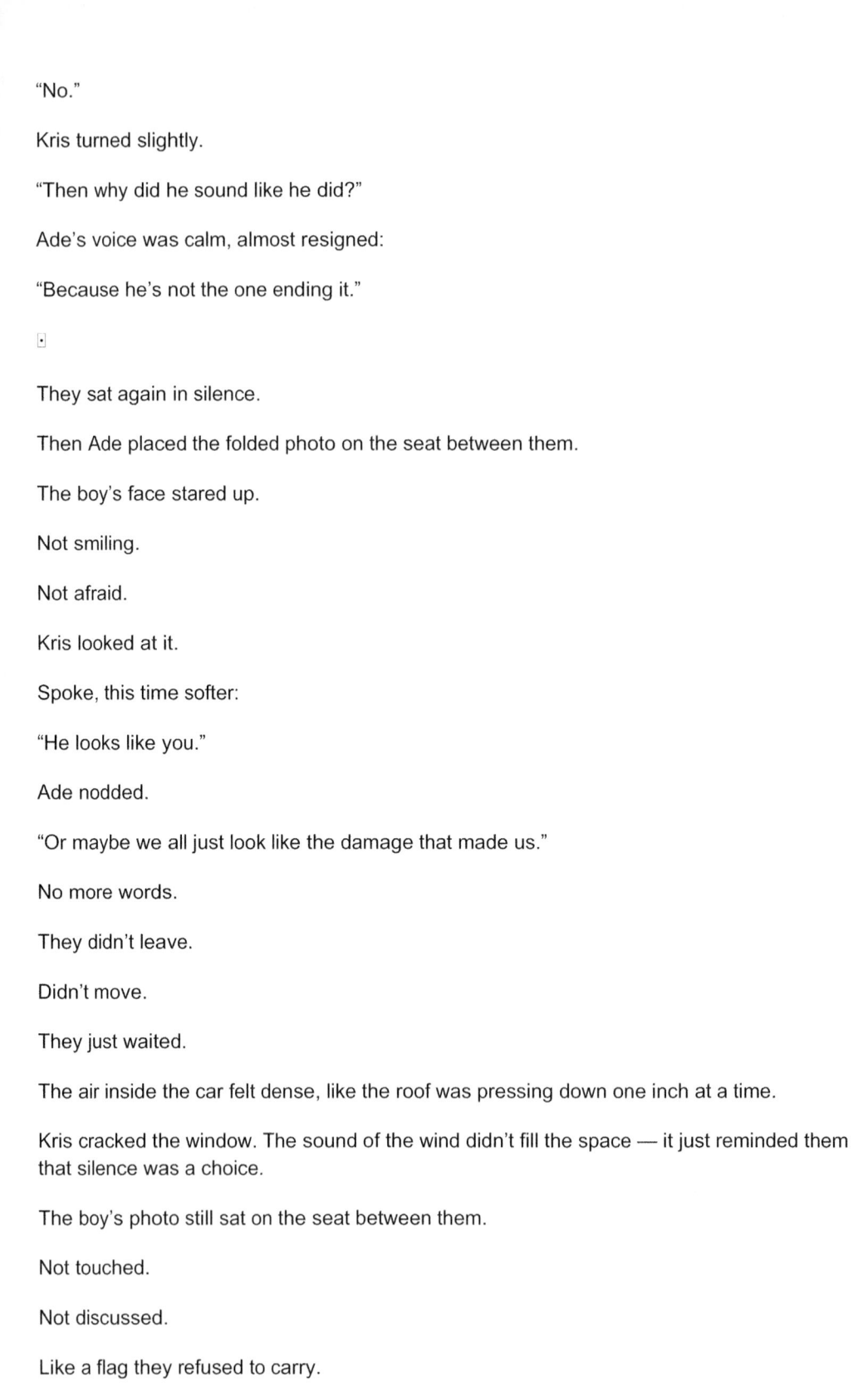

"No."

Kris turned slightly.

"Then why did he sound like he did?"

Ade's voice was calm, almost resigned:

"Because he's not the one ending it."

They sat again in silence.

Then Ade placed the folded photo on the seat between them.

The boy's face stared up.

Not smiling.

Not afraid.

Kris looked at it.

Spoke, this time softer:

"He looks like you."

Ade nodded.

"Or maybe we all just look like the damage that made us."

No more words.

They didn't leave.

Didn't move.

They just waited.

The air inside the car felt dense, like the roof was pressing down one inch at a time.

Kris cracked the window. The sound of the wind didn't fill the space — it just reminded them that silence was a choice.

The boy's photo still sat on the seat between them.

Not touched.

Not discussed.

Like a flag they refused to carry.

Kris finally broke the silence.

"You think we were made for this?"

Ade didn't turn his head.

"No."

"Then why do we keep showing up?"

A pause.

Then Ade said:

"Because it doesn't end unless we're in the room."

Kris gave a slow nod.

Flicked the lighter open.

Closed it.

Open.

Click.

Click.

Click.

"You ever think maybe we weren't the legacy…"

He stared forward.

"…just the leftover noise?"

Ade reached into his pocket, took out the same metal tag Baz once wore — scratched, scorched on one edge.

He held it in his palm like a coin waiting to be spent.

"He kept us talking about fire for so long," Ade murmured. "We forgot what silence feels like."

"Or maybe that was the plan."

Kris looked down at the photo again.

The kid's stare seemed to go through him.

"If the boy becomes what we didn't," he said, "was any of this worth it?"

Ade didn't answer for a long time.

Then:

"If he doesn't, what happens to the fire?"

Another pause.

Kris turned his head slightly.

Looked at Ade fully now.

"I'm tired."

Ade nodded.

Didn't smile. Didn't blink.

Just replied:

"I know."

They sat still.

One breath.

Then another.

No argument.

No escape plan.

No old story rehashed one last time.

Just silence.

The kind that felt final.

Grainy footage.

Monochrome.

Timecode blinking in the corner: 14:37:52.

Camera 2B — northwest pillar, Queen's Cross car park.

The BMW is already there.

Still.

Unmoved for over an hour.

From this distance, the details vanish.

No faces.

No expressions.

Just shadows in the front seats.

Still. Side by side. Unmoving.

⸱

At 14:38:04, a brief flicker — left turn signal flashes once, then dies.

Maybe someone inside shifted.

Maybe someone changed their mind.

⸱

14:39:17 — a spark inside the cabin. Brief. Orange. Likely a lighter.

Then another.

Then a faint glow that doesn't stay lit.

Like a cigarette never quite caught.

⸱

14:40:12 — the rear hazard light clicks on.

Flashes once.

Then again.

Steady.

As if someone's finger held to the dashboard button — not in panic, but with finality.

⸱

And then —

14:40:29

The car vanishes in fire.

No flash.

No warning.

Just eruption — a pressure bloom that punches upward, shattering the overhang above it and peeling back the metal of the surrounding vehicles.

No sound in the footage.

Just the image:

Fire blooming like a flower that hated everything.

The entire screen floods with static as the camera lens fractures.

⸻

Three seconds later, the neighboring feed — Camera 2C — catches the aftermath.

Smoke.

Heat shimmer.

Metal collapsing in on itself.

The car no longer exists.

Not as a shape.

Not as evidence.

Just char and silence.

⸻

No movement.

No one runs in.

No one runs out.

⸻

The next moment captured by any camera is ten minutes later: two security guards in hi-vis scrambling into frame with fire extinguishers too small for the task.

Too late for anything.

Except questions.

⸻

Somewhere, in a high-ceilinged room full of monitors, someone watches the playback again.

Slower this time.

Zoomed in on the moment before the blast.

Fingers pause on the final still frame before combustion.

Two shadows.

Still seated.

Unmoving.

Hands at rest.

One of them had known.

Maybe both.

But the car never moved.

Flashing lights painted the wreckage red and white.

Sirens low — too late, too clean.

The air was thick with smoke, but the heat had already gone.

What was left was ash. And silence. And certainty.

The burnt car was nothing more than a ribcage of metal. No roof. No doors. Just a hollow frame, still steaming.

Two bodies had been inside.

But only one left without a heartbeat.

⸱

A black body bag — scorched, zipped slow — was lifted from the rubble.

Loaded into the back of a coroner's van by men with no rank insignia.

They didn't speak.

They didn't need to.

The world was ending a little differently than they expected.

⸱

Nearby, an ambulance idled.

The stretcher rolled up fast.

One figure, strapped tight.

Oxygen mask. IV line.

Face covered in gauze.

Breathing?

Yes.

But shallow.

One paramedic whispered:

"He's alive."

The other:

"Barely."

No name taken.

Just a tag.

UNKNOWN MALE — HCP, PRIORITY 1

⸺

On a rooftop across the street, Maya watched through binoculars.

Her face unreadable.

Hands still.

She didn't cry.

She didn't exhale.

She simply watched until both vehicles drove away in different directions — one slow and final, the other fast and urgent.

Then she whispered, more to herself than to memory:

"He kept his promise."

⸺

In a safehouse 40 miles outside the city, Drin sat on the edge of a small bed.

The room was dark, save for the glow of the laptop screen in front of him.

On it: the CCTV footage from Camera 2B.

He watched the final three seconds again.

Frame by frame.

Click.

Click.

Click.

Boom.

He didn't flinch.

He didn't rewind.

He just closed the laptop slowly.

Set it aside.

And spoke aloud — to no one:

"Now they'll listen."

Then he stood.

Walked to the window.

Pulled back the curtain.

Outside, a car waited in the fog.

Engine off.

No driver visible.

But the lights blinked once.

Like a signal.

Like confirmation.

Drin didn't wave.

Didn't smile.

He simply let the curtain fall back into place.

And turned toward the dark.

Printed in Dunstable, United Kingdom